BOUND FEET

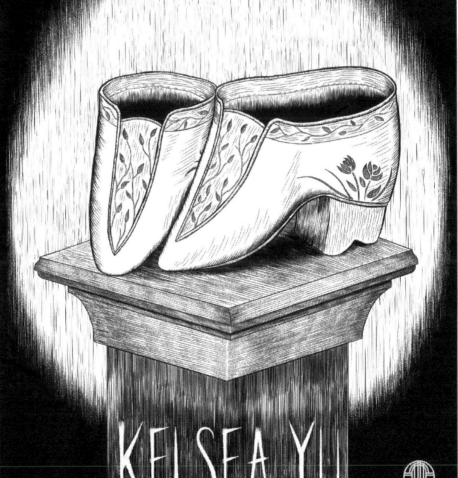

KELSEA YU

CEMETERY GATES
MEDIA

Bound Feet
Published by Cemetery Gates Media
Binghamton, New York

Copyright © 2022
by Kelsea Yu

ISBN: 9798842190188

My Dark Library #3

For more information about this book and other Cemetery Gates Media publications, visit us at:

cemeterygatesmedia.com
twitter.com/cemeterygatesm
instagram.com/cemeterygatesm

Cover Artist and Design: Carrion House

Title page illustration by Ryan Mills

Praise for Kelsea Yu

"Taking us on a thrilling, haunted ride filled with ancient ghosts and startling revelations, *Bound Feet* unveils what must be broken and twisted in order to don the lotus slipper."

—K.P. Kulski, author of *Fairest Flesh*

"Kelsea Yu's *Bound Feet* about a mother's fearlessness, where she reaches into darkness in hopes of grasping light, is a novella carefully plotted and executed without losing realism, heart, or voice of the story. Yu juxtaposes the ancient with the modern, an eerie and jarring inter-section of the past and present that makes everything more uncanny. Yu shows us how loss, grief, and the act of mourning might change you and drive you, taking your mind and body to places you would overwise refuse to enter. A beautiful piece about haunting ghosts who only want their stories told, rather than hidden away, un-finished, untruthful—of friendship, betrayal, lies, and a sisterhood between the living and the dead.

—Ai Jiang, author of *Linghun*

"Grief and folklore intertwine beautifully in this stunning tale. I look forward to reading more from Kelsea Yu!"

—doungjai gam, author of *glass slipper dreams, shattered* and *watch the whole goddamned thing burn*

"Utilizing graceful twists and turns, *Bound Feet* tackles grief and rage passed down through generations. Yu reminds us that the need for not only justice but truth outlives the body."

—J.A.W. McCarthy, author of *Sometimes We're Cruel and Other Stories*

"Haunted by the specters of unimaginable loss, Kelsea Yu's Bound Feet unearths the ways in which past and present can be bound together by the hungry ghosts of violence and betrayal. A story that demands to be heard in more ways than one, the rich reversals and revelations will keep readers on their toes until the very end of this exciting debut."

—Gordon B. White, author of *As Summer's Mask Slips* and *Rookfield*

for my mom,
who taught me kindness.

CONTENTS

FOREWORD

Kelsea Yu's tale begins with the Legend of Portland's Chinese Garden and Ghost Museum. Chapter One tells us that we are at the Gardens in the middle of the night, during a covert operation to sneak onto the grounds, taking place under a full moon.

I immediately fell in love with Kelsea's first-person storytelling voice, Jodi. There's a wholesome, light-heartedness to her persona that makes her feel like a friend. And then there's Jodi's "partner in crime", Sarah.

These two seem like the most unlikely people to be breaking any rules. Here they are, trespassing on private property with only a delicious, picnic meal that is de-scribed in hunger-inducing details and the warm-hearted bond between them.

A friendship formed by shared grief.

Bound Feet is a story centered around every parent's worst fear, the loss of a child.

Knowing this was a major part of the storyline going into it, I felt myself pulling back while I was reading; detaching myself emotionally from the characters so as not to let my heart get broken.

But alas, the prose is too compelling. The characters are altogether endearing and engaging. I helplessly allowed myself to get emotionally attached and it's my hope that you'll open up the secret places of your heart and allow this ghost story to wander in as well. I believe Kelsea Yu will have a long career ahead of her trade-marked by her ability to combine *horror with heart*.

Upon finishing this story, I felt all these feelings bubble to the surface. Mostly, I was just so excited to be given this opportunity to share Kelsea's first published novella. What a gift she has given to the horror community. *Bound Feet* is richly infused with Chinese folklore and culture by way of modern Chinese-American women protagonists, Sarah Xu and Jodi Wu.

I loved the way they honored and wrestled with their heritage openly with each other. For the reader's benefit, it felt welcoming; like we were right there with these two listening to their most intimate conversations.

"The things people will do to keep the systems that oppress them in place." Sarah shakes her head. "All for the fear of change."

For this My Dark Library book, Reader, my hope is for you to find a dark, quiet place where you can fall into this ghost story until you are utterly consumed by the words...

...*Ràng wǒ jìn lái*

Sadie Hartmann
September 2, 2022

*O*n the night of the Hungry Ghost Moon, Zhang Li, a brilliant scholar, was outside burning offerings for his deceased father. As he spoke a prayer, a young lady and her maid strolled past his garden. At once, he was struck by her beauty and found himself utterly captivated. For weeks, he could not eat or drink, and he neglected his studies. His mother grew anxious. Suspecting possession, she hired a Taoist monk to perform an elaborate ritual of exorcism, but despite her efforts, Li began to waste away.

At last, when Li's cousin Wei came to visit, Li's mother implored Wei to extract the truth from her son. Li was despondent at first, but soon he confessed his heartsickness. Wei exclaimed in surprise. "Foolish cousin," Wei laughed pleasantly. "We can easily see your desire fulfilled."

Wei sought out the young lady. After weeks of exhaustive inquiries, he discovered her residence in an adjacent village. Wei promised to make the necessary arrangements, and soon, Li and Ning were married.

Ning was a doting wife, filling Li's table with rich meals, tending his household efficiently, and attending his bed regularly. Yet, as months passed, Li's pallor wanned, and he thinned considerably. When his mother pinched his arm, finding only bone and no meat between her fingers, she sent for a doctor.

"He has been afflicted by a strong ghost presence. His life is being drained away," the doctor told Li's mother. 'The situation is grave. You must rid him of his ghost lover at once.'

Li's mother had grown to love her obedient daughter-in-law. Reluctant to blame Ning, she suspected Li of an affair with a ghost instead and endeavored to catch him so that she could put an end to the matter. But no matter how sharply she guarded her son, he continued to waste away. At last, she admitted to Wei what the doctor had said, and asked him to inquire into the matter.

Wei visited Ning's mother at the cottage where he had made Li and Ning's marital arrangements. When confronted, Ning's mother broke down and told him the truth. Ning had died of a wasting illness before she could marry, *but she had returned as a ghost, determined to find marital bliss.*

Wei returned at once and relayed what he had discovered to his cousin, who had grown so weak now that he was bedridden. Wei implored Li to cast his wife aside. Li summoned Ning to his bedside and in his rage at being tricked, he cursed her for a liar and hit her, before falling back down to his sheets and expiring.

Ning wept and apologized to the corpse of her husband. Fearing Li's family would beat her senseless and cast her out for the grief she had brought them, she quickly confessed to Li's mother that she was pregnant. Li's mother was astonished, for a ghost bride rarely gives children. But it was known to happen on occasion, and Li was her only son. Ning's child was the sole hope for an heir.

To everyone's great joy and surprise, Li and Ning's son was a boy, able to carry on the family name. Having provided an heir, Ning was not punished for her deception, but rather lived on for two decades more. One Ghost Day, Ning left to lay offerings on her mother-in-law's grave and was never seen again.

From the Legend of **Portland's Chinese Garden and Ghost Museum**

CHAPTER 1

Cast in the full moon's ethereal glow, the sheer white walls that enclose Portland's Chinese Garden and Ghost Museum loom before us. My fingers curl around a natural handhold in one of the massive, jagged limestone rocks flanking the iron gate, and I begin to climb.

"I should be the one climbing. It'll take you forever." The breeze carries my best friend's words up to my ears along with a chill that makes my entire body shudder. It stopped raining just before nightfall, but the air is heavy with remembered moisture. Here, atop one of the highest hills in the city, the mid-August wind's bite is redolent of winter.

I roll my eyes, calling down to Sarah. "You're seven months pregnant."

"And I'd still climb faster than you." There's a rustle below as Sarah fidgets with all the gear we packed.

I stifle a laugh. She's one of those health and fitness junkies who thinks a marathon is an enjoyable way to spend a Saturday. The only marathons I'm on board with involve a selection of horror movies and a huge bowl of chips. Sarah is right; she'd probably still beat me up the wall, despite her increasing waistline. But neither of us wants to risk something happening to little baby Henry.

Soon, she'll be a parent.

Again.

I feel around for another secure crevice in the rock, concentrating my energy on the climb ahead to avoid feeding the ugly, jealous beast within me. I'm happy for her. I really am.

When I finally reach the rock's peak, I reach out a tentative hand toward the rounded tiles lining the top of the wall. My probing fingers come back damp, a reminder that I could easily slip off.

Several throaty caws draw my gaze upward to a murder of crows flying overhead, outstretched wings partly obscuring the full moon. They circle back, lower to the ground, and one swoops past so close that I duck and nearly fall in surprise. For one horrible moment, I imagine tumbling to the ground, landing with my neck twisted at just the wrong angle.

"Jodi!" Sarah's voice fills with alarm.

I shake off the image, bracing myself before taking the last step. "I'm fine, I'm fine."

No one's going to die tonight. Not this time.

At the top of the wall, I glance down, instantly regretting the decision as a wave of vertigo hits me. The wall can't be that high, but the garden casts queer shadows that toy with my depth perception. Up here, the breeze howls, warning me not to dawdle. I look around for a safe way down the garden side of the wall, spotting a gnarled tree several yards away. It's spindly, with talon-like branches, but it'll hold my weight. Hopefully.

"Climbing down!" I tell Sarah, who's tapping her feet against the ground below.

"Be careful!"

I scoot over the rounded tiles and test the tree with my foot. It seems solid enough. Cautiously, I climb down, landing on the cement floor tiles with a smack.

It's warmer here, buffered from the wind by the garden's forbidding walls. As I make my way toward the front door, an overgrown weeping willow greets me, its head bowed as if in mourning. Moss peers up through several cracks in the floor; a reminder that no amount of pruning or sweeping can overcome the chaos of nature.

A year has passed since I was last here, but the garden feels the same.

14

An angry part of me simmers with the unfairness. Nothing in my world remained the same after what happened here last Ghost Day; this fateful place should have been changed irrevocably as well.

"Jodi?" Sarah calls. I hear the sound of metal against metal and picture her lifting one of the dramatic lion doorknockers to strike the other side of the rust-streaked door.

"Made it! I'm letting you in now." I move toward the door, fingers crossed that the gate isn't padlocked shut. We brought contingencies in case Sarah needs to climb in, but only as a last resort. In addition to risking her baby's well-being, it would mean throwing our stuff over the wall.

Thankfully, the door unlatches easily from the inside. It creaks open to reveal Sarah with all our gear in tow. I grab my backpack and sleeping bag from her, hefting them onto my shoulders as Sarah crosses the threshold, joining me inside the garden walls.

"You're *sure* those cameras outside aren't on?" Sarah asks.

"Yeah. Got it on good authority," I say, feeling a little guilty at using insider information passed on from my mom, who's friends with one of the garden employees. "They're just deterrents. The owners would rather spend on new exhibits than run a fancy security system. I told you—I've got it covered."

We shut the door behind us and head for the moon gate, a round entrance cut into the wall that separates the entryway from the garden's main body. As we cross through, my head swivels left, eyes seeking the Hungry Ghost Pavilion, where Anton proposed five years ago. I think of the delight in his face when I screamed *yes!*, and my heart clenches.

I haven't seen him smile like that in a year.

Anton must resent me for leaving him alone tonight to go "haring off on another adventure with your weird new friend," as he might have put it if he and I were still on speaking terms. I need to get ahold of my marriage before it slips completely away, but it's so much easier to go thrifting in the Hawthorne District with Sarah, each of us trying to outdo one another in finding the creepiest, vacant-eyed doll. Or to hop in her car for a road trip to Seattle to take the Underground Tour, a 75-minute guided trudge through the city buried beneath the modern-day metropolis.

It was only a month ago that Sarah and I made the switch from daytime to nighttime adventures. As so many things still do, it began with Ella.

One night, when being without Ella was too much to bear, I called Sarah. An hour later, we were sneaking into the graveyard where my baby girl is forever nestled in the ground. Sarah, acting both as friend and lookout, didn't make fun of me for wanting to read Ella her favorite bedtime story or for arranging a tiny blanket in front of the headstone and tucking it into the soil.

Tonight's trip is one more blurring of a line. It's almost like that midnight trip to visit Ella's gravestone. She might not be buried in this garden's soil, but she breathed her last breath here.

"Have you been here before?" I ask Sarah, surprised to learn that I don't know the answer yet. Having a best friend that you've only known for ten months is disorienting, like getting to know someone in reverse. You learn each other's deepest secrets, and then you slowly fill in the rest. It's still surprising to discover the holes in our knowledge of one another.

But it's not Sarah's fault we never talk about the garden.

It takes her so long to respond that I turn to ask again, thinking she didn't hear me. She's stopped, her eyes sweeping the courtyard. Moonlight distorts her expression, but I can see her absorb its quiet beauty. Even in the dim twilight, the majesty of this place can't be denied.

As its name suggests, Portland's Chinese Garden and Ghost Museum is the intertwining of cultures and spaces: part open-air garden, part indoor museum exhibits with an attached teahouse. Like me, the Garden is Chinese American; a marriage of its origins and the place it resides.

"Yes." Sarah responds at last, quiet and thoughtful. "I've been here before. A while ago."

We start walking again, my light step and her confident stride the only human sounds breaking through the sway of leaves, trickle of water, and shuffle of nocturnal wildlife. Stepping along the curved pathways, we pass carefully manicured foliage imported from China.

As I have many times in the past, I wonder what the garden is missing. By nature, the only plants here must grow both in the dreary, wet Pacific Northwest climate, and in the parts of China they were plucked from. What wonders were the garden's owners unable to import? Did they try, only to have the more delicate, climate-shocked flora slowly drown in our unending rainfall?

"I'm glad to see they lit the lotus lanterns tonight," I say as we step onto the jagged wooden walkway that cuts through the garden's large central pond. The white lanterns resemble lotus flowers at the height of their beauty, petals unfurled to reveal little glowing lights that ripple with the waves, like an ever-changing constellation. "It was beautiful last year, fully decorated for the festival."

"Yeah," Sarah says. "I can imagine it was."

"Ella…" I stop, swallowing the painful lump that flares whenever I say my daughter's name. "She loved it here."

Sarah's glance flickers my way, but she doesn't ask if I'm okay. We banned that question from our vocabularies when we first met in person, after many late-night conversations on the Moms Without Kids grief forum. Instead of a question, she pulls my hand into hers, squeezing to let me know she understands. She lost Sean, after all, and three years later, she's still torn up about his death. It's a relief to me, knowing I won't ever get over Ella. I don't ever want to get over my baby girl.

"It looks really peaceful," Sarah says, letting my hand go. "Not like a place that hosts a raucous annual festival."

"It's mine and Anton's fault they're not holding it this year."

Her lips thin, and I can tell she's searching for the right words. She hates it when I blame myself, even as she understands completely. At last, she asks, "Why do you think that?"

"Because Ella's death was the third misfortune to befall the garden."

Sarah's raised eyebrows cut an upside-down v.

"What do you know about the garden's origins?" I ask.

"Not a lot," she admits. "It's been around for decades, right? Since the 90s?"

"Yeah. Though it used to be a regular Chinese garden. Just over four years ago, a new family bought the place and converted it to a ghost garden. But the new owners wanted to bring in something extra; something different. Their daughter was studying Chinese folklore at university and thought it would be cool to theme the garden around ghosts; especially since family lore says they're descended from a ghost."

"Like, real talk they're supposedly part ghost?"

"That's what the stories say. The next part is hearsay, something my mom heard from a friend who heard from her niece who's friends with someone who works at the garden. You know what the Chinese community here is like."

"Recent transplant, remember?"

"Oh, yeah."

She smiles. "New York has gossipy Chinese communities too."

I laugh. "The owners brought in a *qì* expert to consult on the renovations. She warned them against making changes, saying the garden's energy was already in perfect harmony. After some internal family arguments, they ignored her advice and converted it to a ghost garden. They began displaying family heirlooms of their ghost ancestor that they'd brought from China, as well as other ghostly Chinese artifacts they managed to acquire. Their grand re-opening was on Ghost Day four years ago. They planned a huge ghost festival party that got tons of coverage in local papers."

"Sounds fun... and ominous." There's a light popping sound next to me as Sarah leans down to pluck a delicate white flower from a bush.

"Sarah!"

"Oh, it's fine. There are hundreds of these white flowers on this bush alone. It'll be pretty on the altar."

I consider, then pluck my own flower. No way is Sarah's Sean getting an offering that my Ella won't have too. "They decided to move a decorative stone the day of the party that weighed half a ton, so they could set up an extra table for the event."

"Uh oh."

"Yep. While they were transporting the rock, one of the workers slipped in a puddle. The rock fell and crushed his leg. He had to amputate it below the knee."

"Shit, that sounds painful."

"I wasn't there when it happened, of course, but some people swear they can still hear his scream when they cross that part of the garden."

"Which part?"

We're almost to the main building. I point up ahead to the dark corner of the garden, to the left of the teahouse. "Supposedly, somewhere over there, on the pathway by the Venomous Ghost Pavilion."

"Yikes."

Up ahead, I catch a glimpse of the stone footbridge that plagues my dreams each night. I look away hastily, focusing on telling Sarah the story even as my breathing grows strained, like something is clenched around my airway.

"The second Ghost Festival, during the evening tea ceremony, another misfortune befell the garden. While pouring tea for a guest, a dragonfly flew into the server's ear, and she dropped the entire teapot and its boiling contents onto an elderly guest."

"That's horrible."

"He spent a week in the hospital."

Sarah shudders.

I nod, feeling my heartbeat quicken, breaths growing shallow. Far too swiftly, we reach the rounded footbridge over the dark, rippling pondwater.

I stop, squeezing my eyes shut, breath escaping in rapid gasps. I thought I was prepared, but… I can't face this spot. I can't *I can't I can't…*

"Jodi. Take one deep, slow breath. You're okay."

Through the panic, I cling to the firm command in Sarah's calm, steady voice.

Yì bǎi, jiǔ shí jiǔ, jiǔ shí bā…

The power of counting backwards from a hundred in Mandarin feels weak against the rushing tide of everything, but it's enough to anchor me. Sarah's hand slips into my own, her light, soft touch incongruous with my clammy grip.

I cling to the numbers, taking long, deep breaths until my racing heartbeat slows back down. When it finally resembles a normal pace again, I give Sarah's hand a squeeze to let her know I'm ready. In unison, we step onto the bridge. As we cross, my attention is drawn by a flash of movement at the edge of my vision.

Wonder pushes the lingering panic out of my system as I watch the mesmerizing dance of multicolored koi swirling through the water, rising up as if to eat at the surface.

"They look hungry," Sarah says.

"Almost as if they expect a midnight snack."

"Maybe they eat visitors who trespass on the garden at night."

We both giggle, and I marvel at her ability to help me snap out of a mood. My eye catches the spot where… where…

I sober up. "She drowned beneath this bridge." I feel Sarah's grip tighten in mine. "I thought Anton was watching her and he thought I was and… somehow she ended up there, alone, drowning in two feet of water." I wait for the sharp words to cut through my chest, but the pain is mild. Nothing could possibly be worse than being here, in the place where my little girl died of neglect while I laughed and drank with friends.

"That was the third… misfortune?" Sarah asks, and I nod. We begin moving forward again, curving around the pond.

"The owners didn't want to wait around for the unlucky fourth event, so they abandoned the Ghost Day celebration this year, leaving the garden closed."

In Mandarin, the word for four sounds similar to the word for death. I don't need to explain the superstition about the number four to Sarah; she's Chinese, like me, though her family is from mainland China and mine is from Taiwan. Sarah Xu and Jodi Wu.

"Is this where you want to set up?" Sarah asks as we come back around to the shore near the stone footbridge.

"Yeah. I want to perform the ritual out here, near the spot where she…" I swallow the lump in my throat. "…near the bridge."

"You don't want to do this inside?" Sarah asks, gesturing toward the big building at the heart of the garden, a two-story museum and teahouse, in the style of classic Chinese architecture.

I gulp. "No. Ghost Day rules warn against lighting the altar inside, lest we invite um… *hǎo xiōng dì jiě mèi* in."

"*Hǎo xiōng dì jiě mèi*? Good… brothers and sisters?"

I wince. "I read online that we're not supposed to call them you know… the g-word, out loud. It's bad luck or something."

"But you just said Ghost Day."

"Yeah. I thought it was interesting, but it's not like I really believe the superstitions anyway." Probably.

Sarah doesn't believe in ghosts. She finds folklore conceptually fascinating because it's often a helpful historical record in understanding the lives of everyday people, but she doesn't think the supernatural elements in the tales are real.

I, on the other hand, am not so sure. But I figure that even if the ritual amounts to nothing, it feels right to be here. We'll spend an hour or two checking out the property and telling each other ghost stories, without the interference of other meddlesome humans. Then, if it feels right, we'll eat the food we brought and talk about the kids that were taken from us far too soon, before we fall asleep in the beautiful teahouse. In the morning, we'll clean everything and sneak back out.

Coming here was my idea, and I've done all the research for this trip. Sarah was unsure at first, but I think she eventually agreed to it because she thinks it's better for me to do something active instead of sitting around hating myself extra hard tonight. She's a good friend.

"Okay," Sarah says. "Let's get started then."

Gratefulness warms me as I begin laying out the contents of my backpack. Carefully, I unwrap a set of plastic dragon-printed plates I got one Lunar New Year and hand them to Sarah. She takes a stack of blue-topped Tupperware out of her bag and begins arranging the food. Next, I set up the two portable altars, shaped like tiny Chinese temples, that I bought in Chinatown. One for Ella, one for Sean. Beneath my altar's roof, I place the white blossom besides a candle and a framed photo of Ella, smiling on her third—and last—birthday.

We breathe in the salty, delicious scent as Sarah pours soy sauce over the *chángfěn*. My mouth waters at the rice noodle rolls wrapped around fried shiitakes and scallions, but I resist taking a bite. This food is meant for the dead. Sarah's kept some of each dish in the Tupperware for our midnight meal; we'll eat it warm if we can find a way to heat it up.

She opens up the next container and I gasp, marveling at the pointed peach-shaped rice cakes inside. They're encased in a gelatinous rosy layer, lucky pink covering up the inauspicious white of the rice beneath. She uses chopsticks to place several on a plate.

"Sarah, those look perfect!" They look exactly like the rice cakes at last year's festival, down to the stylized symbol for longevity stamped into each cake. "Were they hard to make?"

"Thanks," she says, smiling. "They weren't too tough. I found a recipe online."

"Which means I would've mangled them badly."

Sarah snorts a laugh, but doesn't disagree, probably remembering the time I accidentally put salt in a batch of cookies... instead of sugar. She lines another plate with orange slices and peeled lychee, Ella's and Sean's respective favorite fruits, as I arrange the elements of her altar. Next to each kid's photo, I place a jar of incense. As Sarah pours milk from a thermos into two little cups, I tear open a package of thin white papers with metallic squares in the center.

Above us, gray clouds shift, filtering parts of the full moon through a hazy mask. Light reflects off the water in waves. Leaves rustle and somewhere unseen, a bird trills a lonely night song. Cast in the glow of the lanterns, the garden air around us feels full of potential.

Like anything is possible.

I dig out the lighter from my backpack's front pocket and hand Sarah half the stack of joss paper. "Ready?"

"Almost," she says, opening one last container to reveal two fortune cookies.

My throat feels tight and my eyes sting as appreciation surges through me.

"Thank you," I whisper. Months ago, I told Sarah how much Ella loved snapping open fortune cookies and making up barely comprehensible, nonsensical fortunes for everyone, giggling as she told them to me and Anton.

Sarah places the fortune cookies on the edge of the fruit platter, and nods.

I light Ella's candle, then the incense sticks around us and the joss paper, setting it on the altar to burn. Sarah takes the lighter from my hand, following suit as spicy sandalwood fills the air. In Mandarin, we both recite blessings for our ancestors and offer them an invitation to the feast.

For the next prayer, I squeeze my eyes shut. I put every ounce of will into my thoughts, as if I could force the universe to obey my wishes. Praying to anything—any-one—out there.

Please, Ella, come back to Mama. Mama misses you. Mama loves you. Please. I would do anything, give anything to see you one more time.

Anything.

CHAPTER 2

When I open my eyes again, a tear escapes, and I see that Sarah's cheeks glisten. I know she's thinking of her little boy, Sean, forever trapped at age two.

Sarah takes a deep, trembling breath before her shiitake-brown irises greet mine. Our gazes lock. Her lips part, and the yearning in her face leaves me breathless and wondering. Despite her stance as a seasoned skeptic, has she let herself believe that the ritual might have worked? Have I?

Our gazes tear apart as we both look around the garden, ears alert. I hold on to hope, reminding myself that belief is easy when it asks only for the brief length of a wish; the difficulty lies in the sustaining.

But it's hard to fight the sinking feeling as we gaze across the courtyard, our rapacious eyes seeking any sign that we're in a different world than we were before the ritual.

Nothing.

I get to my feet and start walking along the path.

"Jodi, what are you doing?"

Going to find my baby girl.

"Looking around," I say.

Sarah's teeth dig into her bottom lip, and I know that whatever momentary belief she might have carried, it's already gone.

With Sarah by my side, I'm too self-conscious to call out for Ella. Instead, I carry thoughts of her in my mind, hoping they'll draw her to me, somehow. Ella, smiling and running toward me on this pathway. *"Mama! Daddy says we can get a mooncake today!"* Ella, snuggling close to me at night as I read her favorite Chinese New Year picture book aloud. Ella, whispering that she loves me right before falling asleep.

We check all three pavilions. We walk all around the main building, peer behind every rock or bush, weave through the densest thicket of trees. I look past the lotus lanterns into the pond's murky depths, which appear far deeper than possible in the peculiar lighting of the full moon. I look for two round pink cheeks, but all I see in the water is the reflection of my own haggard, desperate face.

Ghost Day is supposed to be the one day of the year when spirits can reach our world.

But everything is fine. I didn't really believe anything would happen tonight.

I *didn't*.

At last, when Sarah has indulged me long enough, we end our silent traipse through the garden, returning to the altars. We kneel down to pick up the containers of food saved for our own feast. Sarah snaps a lid shut. The sound echoes through the night air, feeling irreversibly final.

My vision blurs. I fight tears, but they pour out faster than I can wipe them away. I swear the taunting scents of Ella's favorite foods grow stronger as I cry. "Let's just go drop our stuff off." My voice chokes as I pick up a stack of Tupperware. "Then we can check out the exhibits."

As I stand up, my hand reaches out to brush the framed photo of Ella, wanting to bring it with me. We're keeping the altars up and feast out for the ghosts as long as we're here; it's part of the reason we decided to stay overnight. But I can't help feeling like I'm leaving my baby girl out in the cold.

"Give me a hint of what's in the museum," Sarah says, tone light. "They've gotta have some pretty weird things on display."

"Hm." I take Sarah's verbal opening and grasp at it, as I have many times before, letting her pull me out of my melancholy. I think back to the various artifacts encased inside the building. "Ooo, you *have* to see the human bench."

"Um, please tell me that is not a bench made of person?"

"Depends who you ask."

Sarah shudders. A laugh escapes my throat, and she gives me a sidelong smile. We skip the museum's front door, opting instead for a path that leads directly into the teahouse at the back of the main building. Sarah jiggles the lacquered wooden doors. "They're locked."

I pull out the lockpicks I bought online.

"Do you have *any* idea what you're doing?" Sarah asks.

"Sure. I'm a YouTube-tutorial-certified lockpicker."

"I don't think *lockpicker* is a word."

"Spoken like a lockpicker-wannabe. It's part of the lockpicking lingo."

Sarah huffs a laugh as the door clicks open. "Alright, you win. You are the official lockpicker of our duo."

I frown. "Are you sure they were locked? I don't think I actually did anything. I think it was already open."

"Oh, come on," Sarah says. "Why would they leave it unlocked?"

"Maybe because they figure the walls keep people out anyway?"

"Maybe." Sarah shrugs.

Or maybe something else has decided it wants us here.

I blink away the bizarre thought, pulling the door open. "Don't question a good thing, right?"

As the door swings toward us, a wave of warm air passes over me. It's thick and cloying, with a slight sweatiness to it, and I swear I can hear flies buzzing lethargically. My mind flashes back to a decade-old memory of stepping out of the plane into Xi'an on a family trip; the shock of realizing we were in a whole new world.

This isn't Pacific Northwest air.

Sarah coughs. "What was that?"

"A draft?" Even to my own ears, the words aren't convincing. I step inside briskly. "Come on."

The teahouse greets us, filled with lacquered wooden tables and benches, patterns carved into their marrow. I close my eyes for a moment. All around me sit the ghosts of last *Zhōng Yuán Jié* when the teahouse was brimming with guests and laughter.

"Should we set up here?" Sarah suggests. "We can move some of the tables."

"Sure. This spot is perfect."

Together, Sarah and I move a table and some chairs, carving out a nice corner for our sleepover. My forest green sleeping bag crinkles loudly as it unrolls; Sarah's thinner purple bedroll unfurls more quietly. I tuck my travel blanket and thin pillow inside my sleeping bag; hopefully, they'll warm up a bit. We put the food in the fridge, except for two rice cakes, which Sarah sets on the counter. "Ready?"

"Yeah!"

Sarah hands me a rice cake to snack on along the way. I bite into it, savoring the delicious flavor of rice stir fried with shallots, garlic and peanuts as I reach for my phone, before remembering that I left it at Sarah's place. Anton and I have "find my friend" turned on, and he thinks I'm sleeping over there. I doubt he cares enough to check, but I'd rather not take the risk. Sarah has her phone in case of emergency, but I packed a bright yellow flashlight; a panic purchase after our power went out for days when Ella was half a year old.

Sarah's phone light and my flashlight cut uneven patterns through the darkness as we munch on rice cakes, weaving our way deeper into the teahouse toward the entrance to the hallway. I walk quickly by the spot where I was sitting as my baby drowned, wrestling back the self-loathing that looms up as we pass. Ahead of me, Sarah slides open the door.

The corridor to the main exhibit hall glows; moon-light streams in through the intricate scroll work cut into each of the wooden shutters lining the walls, rendering our artificial light unnecessary. We keep our lights on anyway, clinging to the illusion of control, as if the talismans we hold act as adequate guards against the kinds of things that lurk at night.

I see the flash of a face ahead and jump back, crashing into Sarah, before realizing it's only her reflection staring back at us from the Ghost Mirror; one of the exhibits on display.

"Jesus, you're jumpy," she says.

"Yeah, something about this place feels... you know." I shiver. "Haunted."

"We're in a fucking *ghost museum* at night on the one day of the year when ghosts are supposed to be able to reach our world. Of course, it feels creepy. That's the point."

I laugh half-heartedly. "Yeah, I know. I know."

"Don't wimp out on me now."

"I'm not!" I race ahead to the first exhibit, annoyed with myself for being such an easy scare. "Let's see what we have here. Oh, this one is new! I mean, it's really fucking old, but it's new since last time I was here."

"What is it?" Sarah peers over my shoulder, so close that her warm breath tickles my ear. "Is that *dirt*?"

I giggle, squinting at the gold plaque. "Not just any old dirt. This is soil straight from a family courtyard in China, where the Spitting Ghost's bones were said to have been buried, putting her to rest."

"Um, what is the Spitting Ghost?"

I turn to her and hold the flashlight under my chin, casting my face in an ethereal glow. "The Spitting Ghost was the young wife of a well-to-do magistrate. She displeased her husband by overcooking a dish of long-life noodles on his birthday. In recompense, her eyes were gouged out by official decree. She died from improper post-gouge medical care. Enraged by the injustice, she stuck around in the afterlife and spit acid into his eyeballs, melting them painfully. He ran into the hills, screaming until he lost his voice, and was eaten by a tiger."

"You're so full of shit."

I flick Sarah's cheek. "Try to top it, then."

"Fine. Give me the flashlight." She pulls it from my hands and copies me, clearing her throat dramatically before speaking. "The story of the Spitting Ghost begins with a tiny, mischievous cricket."

"I'm getting Mulan vibes."

She swats at me. "Stop interrupting! As I was saying, this cricket was rather intelligent. It was stealthy and persistent, and it could speak the local human language. Every night for three years, the cricket snuck into the ear of the lead chef of the regional army commander, whispering that he should spit in the food to make it tastier."

I imagine the cricket's little antennae probing inside my ear canal and resist the urge to pick at my ear. No way will I let Sarah see me react visibly to her story. "Do crickets even live that long?"

"It's a *magical* cricket, duh. Finally, the cricket's persistence paid off. The chef began spitting in the commander's food, mixing in his loogies with the sauce. Thinking itself hilarious, the cricket sat and watched from its perch in the chef's hair. When the commander found out, he had the chef boiled alive. The order was carried out so swiftly that the cricket didn't have a chance to escape unseen, and it was boiled alive too. They died together. Now man and cricket wander the netherworld, the man spitting into everyone's food while the cricket whispers in his ear."

"He was *boiled alive?* Well, that's a horrible story."

"Yeah, and your eye gouging, man-eaten-by-tiger story was a real treat."

I snort. "Fine, we can listen to the real story and see whose was closer."

We open another sliding door to the entryway and ticket booth area, where a set of audio guides hangs on a stand. I pass one to Sarah and take another for myself, place the headphones over my ears. Sarah does the same as we walk back to the dirt display. I type in the number next to the headphones symbol on the plaque, and a disembodied voice whispers into my ear.

"One night, in the abode of a scholar who had recently passed the Second Examination, the lady of the household heard strange, repetitive noises from her private courtyard. Curious, she peeked out from behind her screen to spy a figure at the far end of the yard. It had white hair done in a topknot and it pranced around the courtyard like a crane, spitting jets of water. The outside air smelled foul and the lady quickly hid back inside again. Astonished, she called for her two attendants, who witnessed the same odd spectacle. They warned her against letting the ghost see her, hurriedly shuttering the doors and hunching below the screen.

"As the spitting noises grew louder and the stench stronger, the lady's curiosity won out. She wanted a closer look at the ghost who dared haunt her courtyard. With her two attendants cowering in fear, the lady sprang up from the floor and flung open the shutters.

"The elderly ghost turned toward her, eyes clouded over, face wrinkly as a dried plum, and leered. She spat a great stream of foul water onto the lady's face. The attendants screamed and gagged as the water landed on their mistress. It burned away skin and meat wherever it touched, revealing portions of her skull still staring out into the courtyard in shock.

"The lady died, and the ghost was never seen again. They buried the lady and mourned her. Years later, when the scholar's new wife had the spot in the center of the courtyard dug up to plant a new bush, servants uncovered the body, seemingly intact, of an elderly woman. As soon as she was exposed to air, her skin began to rot away, and they found her entire body was filled with the most foul-smelling water.

"The dirt before you comes from the courtyard of the Spitting Ghost. The soil of the courtyard has been completely infertile since the Spitting Ghost's body disintegrated into it."

Sarah taps me on the shoulder and I jump up, the storyteller's mesmerizing voice causing me to nearly forget where I am. Sarah's right. I *am* jumpy today.

I pull off my headphones. "That story was even more disgusting than yours."

Sarah laughs. "Think this dirt really contains essence of ghost?"

Sarah lifts the flashlight and we inspect the display closely, as if the old ghost's wrinkly hand might pop out at any moment. The soil does look crumbly and pale, as if something had sucked it dry of nutrients. "Who knows. It's probably some dirt from a desert or something."

"I'm sure the museum owners wouldn't do that," Sarah says, and I raise my eyebrow at her. She rolls her eyes. "I believe the best in people until proven otherwise."

"Bold words from someone currently trespassing," I say, smiling.

She laughs. "This is different! We'll clean everything in the morning and won't damage anything; they'll never need to know. Anyway, I judge by my own particular set of standards, partner in crime."

We weave through several exhibits, listening to the artifacts' respective stories. I delight in telling Sarah about the much-anticipated human bench, which is supposedly from a haunted house in China. One day, the owner sat on his garden bench, noting it was too soft and pliable... and sure enough, it had turned briefly into a bench-shaped thing with human parts. He ran off screaming. When he finally dared return, the bench was back to normal, but he put it in storage and never sat on it again.

"I want to sit on the bench now," Sarah declares.

"Why?"

"Maybe it only turns into a person with the warmth of someone's butt."

"And that's a reason *to* sit on the bench?"

She shrugs. "It would be interesting, anyway."

After we've circled the edges of the room, we reach the center, where the main displays lie. Sarah walks briskly ahead of me, pulling off her navy sweater in one swift motion. Her t-shirt clings to it and I catch a glimpse of her tanned belly, skin stretched thin by the fetus growing inside her, and the hint of underwire covered in black lace, before she pulls down her t-shirt. "Guess what's in this display?" Sarah's cheeks flush rosy-pink as she holds her sweater over the glass and hums a dramatic tune. "Dun dun dun dun…"

From my numerous visits here before Ella's death, I already know what's behind the cloth, but I play along, trying to ignore my rapidly beating heart as my fingers tap out a drum roll on the nearest wall.

She swipes her sweater away for the grand reveal.

"It's… a really old vase!"

I laugh and join her, our elbows touching as we lean in. My nose presses against the glass, leaving behind a smudge mark when I step back. I reach out to wipe it away with my sleeve, but Sarah stops me.

"What are you, afraid they'll ID you based on your nose?"

I scoff. "It just feels wrong to smudge this pristine glass."

She leans forward to press her nose against the glass too, her slightly wider nose-print resting next to mine. Her forehead bumps the surface, leaving yet another print.

I smile. "They'll arrest us together. Didn't you hear? Nose prints and forehead prints are the newest investigation techniques. All the rage."

She flicks the end of my nose. "We'll have to burn the tips of our noses and my forehead so that they can't prove anything."

"Yeah, that'll be really inconspicuous." I laugh, turning back toward the exhibit to look at the plaque, as if I didn't already have this one memorized. "It's the story of the owner's ancestor, Ning. Supposedly, her ashes are in this urn."

Sarah stops in the middle of pulling her headset on. "Oh yeah?"

"The museum was founded by a married couple. The husband wrote down the story of his great great who-knows-how-many greats grandparents, which had been passed down through the generations. According to the legend, his ancestor, Ning, was a ghost who tricked a man into marrying her, and then slowly sucked the life out of him, through sex, until he died."

Sarah bursts out laughing, the lively sound echoing loud and clear through the empty hallway. "Wait, are you joking?"

I can't help grinning in return. "For real. They carefully allude around that in the tale, but yeah."

Sarah shakes her head. "It is funny how much sex shows up in ancient Chinese folktales. I mean, it's not really funny since the context is almost always disgustingly misogynistic. But it's interesting. Of course, there were all sorts of monstrous things women were suspected to be, back then. I secretly hope that the part about him slowly dying was true, but it's because Ning poisoned his meals or something."

"I hope you're right, and Ning is a total badass. Because the alternate is that she's probably just another girl married off as a teen to an entitled prick whose story somehow turned into a pretty legend, probably after she died some horrible death."

"Yeah."

"Hey, does that mean you've been reading up on Chinese folklore?" I ask. Sarah has mentioned wanting to read folklore someday, but as far as I know, she hasn't had the chance yet.

Sarah blinks. "Not really. Just a few essays on the subject and a story that came up in a podcast. Alright, you have me curious. I *have* to hear the full legend now." She puts her headset back on.

I follow suit and we listen to Ning's story.

"On the night of the Hungry Ghost Moon..."

A few minutes in, something rustles from outside. With my headset on, I can't tell exactly where it's coming from. Maybe somewhere behind me? I glance over at Sarah, who's fully absorbed in the tale. Not wanting to call attention to what is probably mere paranoia, I slowly walk around the display, as if studying all angles of the urn. When I've turned enough that I'm facing the part of the garden where I think I heard the noise. Surreptitiously, I turn down the volume on my headphones and scan the landscape outside, heart pounding.

There's nothing out there.

I swallow a disappointed lump in my throat and pace back and forth, stopping every few steps to glance around. The voice in my headset continues to whisper, and I catch the part where Li's mother calls in a doctor to check on her son.

Mama?

Every muscle in my body tenses when I hear the voice, a faint echo. Am I imagining things?

Mama?

My head snaps up toward the garden. My heart speeds up as I see the blurry, formless shape of *something* out there, but through the delicately latticed windows, I can't make out more than a vague outline.

My mouth goes dry. Ella?

Bone-cold fingers wrap around mine and I shriek, pulling my hand up so fast I knock the headset half-off my head and in righting it, drop my flashlight. It instantly goes out.

"Jesus, Jodi!" Sarah stares at me, wide-eyed. "What the fuck?"

My heart beats so loudly that I'm almost surprised she can't hear it, a rhythmic pounding in my ears...

"Jodi, snap out of it!" Sarah snaps her fingers in my face, and I blink.

"I... thought I heard something. And then saw something in the garden."

Sarah follows my gaze out through the window, but whatever was there a minute ago is gone. "Wow, dude. This place is really getting to you, isn't it?"

"Uh, *no it's not.* I um... there was a sound."

"Yeah, I heard it too."

My attention snaps back to Sarah. "You did?"

"Duh? The ghost tour has sound effects as part of the audio. It's a ghost museum. It's supposed to be creepy."

My heart sinks so low and heavy that I think it's going to drag me beneath the floorboards. "They didn't have that when I was here last year."

"Maybe they added it recently."

"It wasn't a sound from the audio." My words sound petulant and childish.

Sarah shrugs. "If you say so."

I reach down to pick up the flashlight, pressing the button to no effect. "And the timing of the light going out is strange. I've barely used this flashlight. Aren't these things supposed to be super durable?"

"The battery probably ran out," Sarah says, always the practical one. "Or the flashlight sat in some warehouse for years before you purchased it. Or maybe they gave you an old battery to start with."

"Maybe."

Whenever we end up discussing the possible existence of the supernatural, Sarah starts digging her heels in. I can tell there's no point in arguing with her right now, so I don't bother. She can cling to her stubborn beliefs if she wants. She didn't hear what I heard.

It wasn't a random noise. I'm attuned to the sound of Ella calling for me, and *that was her.*

My annoyance with Sarah fades as I realize what this means.

Ella called for me.

Somehow, the ritual actually worked. It worked. It worked it worked it *worked!*

I know Sarah won't believe me without hard evidence, but I don't need her belief.

My baby is here... and I need to find her.

CHAPTER 3

These days, Sarah is the only person whose presence usually relaxes me, but right now, being in the room with her feels stifling. The heart-shaped hope budding within me is still too fragile, too easily broken. It wants to stay hidden until it has the chance to grow stronger. It wants space.

"I'm going to find the restroom," I say.

"Want me to come with you?"

"Nah, I'm fine," I walk off before she can say anything else.

The bathroom, with its bamboo sink and single toilet enclosed in a decorative, lacquered screen, is colder than the rest of the teahouse and smells vaguely of disinfectant. I lean against the wall and close my eyes for a moment, imagining a familiar face materializing from the shapeless form out in the dark. Two rows of crooked baby teeth arranged in a grin beneath a small button nose, and amber eyes looking straight at me.

Shhh, Mama. I'm hiding from the scary lady.

I gasp and open my eyes again as footsteps near the entrance. Quickly, I turn the faucet on and splash water on my face. Through the mirror, I see Sarah appear in the doorway. I turn the water off, composing myself.

"You look like you've seen a..." Sarah breaks off, a smile creeping onto her face. "Never mind. Everything alright?"

I grab a towel and wipe water off my skin. "Yeah. I'm *fine*. God, you're such a helicopter mo..."

Oh, fuck.

Sarah's face falls for a moment before she knits her features back into place. I want to smack myself. How could I have been so thoughtless, knowing she berates herself every day for not watching Sean closely enough the day he fell off the balcony of a seaside vacation rental? I remember Sarah's words from our first conversation. *People always say helicopter parent like it's a bad thing. But if I could go back and redo one thing in this world, I'd be a fucking helicopter mom every moment of every day.*

I try not to think of her little boy, body splattered on the rocks lining the beach below the bungalow.

"I'm an asshole," I say.

"Stop it." Steel enters Sarah's voice as she waves me off. "It's not a big deal." She pushes past me into the bathroom stall. I remember what it was like to be seven months pregnant. You have to pee all the fucking time.

When Sarah emerges, her public face is back on. I don't push; I've seen her without her mask in place, but it's not always a matter of whom else is in the room. Sometimes your *I'm fine* shield isn't for anyone but yourself.

I force a laugh. "Come on. You have to see the scroll and Ning's slippers."

We head back to the exhibit room and I beeline for the display case just beyond the urn.

I point to the huge scroll behind the glass case. It's a 19th-century Chinese illustration accompanied by brush-painted characters; I've spent countless hours here, inspecting the style and details. Inevitably, my eyes travel down to a figure standing in the inner courtyard of her home. Her hair is pinned up in an elaborate style, topped with a decorative phoenix comb, and her robes are richly embroidered with wide, draping sleeves. "That's Ning. Or at least Ning as the artist that her grandson commissioned imagined her, based on descriptions he'd been told."

"Whoa," Sarah leans closer to inspect the drawing. "This is so cool!"

"Yeah, I love this painting. They have her slippers here, too." I point toward the bottom of the display. Two emerald green, heavily embroidered slippers sit propped up behind the glass, tipped forward for our viewing pleasure.

Sarah laughs. "Those look like toy shoes! They have to be replicas. No one's feet are that small."

"Hers were. Because she had bound feet."

Sarah gasps. "Oh my god. I always forget about that."

"I can't forget," I say softly. "My great grandma had bound feet."

As a kid, I didn't understand *Ah Zòu*'s triangular feet. I'd asked why she only had one toe, and she lifted up her foot to show me the rest. Every toe except the biggest one on each foot had been broken before her fourth or fifth birthday and bound tightly underneath with a long cloth. They were kept compressed as she grew. By the time she reached adulthood, they were badly misshapen, pressed into the underside of her feet and causing her lifelong pain.

All so her feet could be stuffed into impossibly tiny lotus shoes.

"Wow. I don't know if I've ever seen an illustration of them," Sarah says. Her eyes linger on the drawing. The little bump of Ning's foot being pushed up to unnatural heights by the toes crushed underneath.

"It's fucked up," I say. "And yet, it was the women who fought hardest when foot binding was finally outlawed."

"They probably thought their daughters and grand-daughters wouldn't find husbands without bound feet. Marriage: the end all be all, back in the day."

"Maybe," I say softly. "But from what I've read, I think it went beyond that. Putting themselves and their daughters through the immense pain of foot-binding gave them a chance to demonstrate their devotion to Confucian values and the male-dominated hierarchy of the dynastic system. It was a way of upholding the crumbling world around them."

"The things people will do to keep the systems that oppress them in place." Sarah shakes her head. "All for the fear of change."

"Sure," I say. "Something like that."

After a few more minutes looking at the details of the illustration, I turn to ask Sarah if she's done with the exhibits. Her eyes travel down the scroll, top to bottom, right to left.

"You can read *fán tǐ zì*?" Surprise lifts my voice. Sarah is mainland Chinese, and traditional *hàn yǔ* characters haven't been part of mainland Chinese curriculum since the 1950s, when Simplified was formally adopted.

"Yeah! My grandpa taught me. He's kind of a snob about it. Did you learn *jiǎn tǐ zì*?"

I stiffen, my shame at not being Chinese enough rising to the surface. "I... can't read any Chinese characters. Only *pīnyīn*." And my limited knowledge of *pīnyīn*, Chinese words written in the Romanized alphabet with tonal accents, was sussed out from my knowledge of the spoken language. I never learned *pīnyīn* formally.

"Ah," she says, oblivious to my embarrassment. "I haven't finished Ning's story yet. It's almost more fun trying to read the rest from the scroll, though some of these characters are pretty archaic." She squints at one of the words before putting the headphones back on and pressing play. The muffled sounds of the narration leak out through her headset.

With Sarah distracted once more, I look back out to the garden, but the blurry shape isn't there. I think about Ella's words. *I'm hiding from the scary lady.*

Soon, Ella. Mama's going to come find you. Right after I make sure Sarah's safely tucked away first.

When Sarah's done listening, we wipe the headsets off and put them back carefully before returning to the teahouse. Neither of us is hungry, so we leave our food in the fridge; we can eat it in the morning. I slip into the silky comfort of my sleeping bag as Sarah nestles into her bag, within arm's reach. She adjusts her blankets and then turns to face me, black tresses spilling out behind her as her cheek presses into her pillow.

"I wonder what life was like for Ning," she says.

"Same," I say. "The story is so one-sided. Li saw her walking one night and decided she was so beautiful he *had* to have her as his wife. Did she have any say in the matter?"

"Girls really didn't have it great in ancient China."

"Sadly, I don't think that was limited to China."

Sarah grunts agreement, yawning. She closes her eyes and I do the same, but I pinch my leg, determined not to let myself succumb to the dreamy, sleep-inducing moonlight. When she speaks again, it's in the soft haze of the half-awake. "Did you know my dad was disappointed I was a girl?"

I draw in a sharp breath. "What?"

Sarah doesn't like to talk about her family, and the two of us always meet up without others around. I don't know a lot about them. "Yeah," she says, barely a whisper. For a moment, I wonder if she's fallen asleep. Then her eyes flutter open to look at me. She smiles, a pretty wisp of a thing that fills my heart with love, hurt, and something else. "He wanted me to carry on the family name. And he's never stopped blaming me for Sean. I think my dad is angrier at me for Sean's death, because he was a boy." Her eyelids flutter closed again.

I let Sarah sleep again, heart heavy imagining my beautiful, brilliant best friend being made to feel not good enough because she's a girl. At least none of my family has ever blamed me for Ella.

Not aloud, anyway.

But it's in every simmering interaction between me and Anton. I've screamed at him, told him I hated him almost as much as I hated myself, told him Ella's death was our fault and that we would never, ever be able to redeem ourselves. Meanwhile, in the face of my roaring rage, Anton went the opposite; stubbornly quiet. Bull-headed in his insistence on not blaming me. But I can see it in every look, every time he sets the pot on the stove a little too hard, the way he no longer waits for me to eat dinner.

I keep my eyes closed, feigning rest, but every so often I check on Sarah's progress as she falls asleep facing me. The strangely intimate gesture of trust is another reminder of what Anton and I no longer have. My chest suddenly fills with hurt as I think of the way he turns away from me every night, leaving me to stare at his broad back as his breaths slowly level out. As he escapes to the only world where anything is still possible.

Anton and I put all of our love into Ella, and then we killed her with our neglect.

The light, nasal whine of Sarah's snores drift into the air. I watch for several minutes until I'm sure she's deep enough asleep.

Wraith-like, I slip out into the crisp night.

A tender breeze caresses my arms as I step onto the garden path, heading for the spot where the figure stood. On the pathway, I pass by one of the dormant cherry blossom trees and reach out to brush its bark with my fingertips. A curled piece of bark falls off the branch too easily, and for a moment, I wish I hadn't missed this spring's Cherry Blossom Festival.

Growing up, I learned all the fanciful stories about the garden—back when it was the Chinese Garden and Tea-house; before the new owners converted it to a ghost garden. As a child, I spent one fruitless week trying to verify my favorite tale: in late winter, it is said that precisely ten thousand plum blossoms flower all across the courtyard. Last January, I told Ella that tale as we ducked beneath the smallest tree, branches covered with flesh-pink, five-petaled flowers in full bloom.

As I pull my arm back from the bare branch, my palm itches with the memory of an illicit blossom she plucked and placed in my hand.

You're prettier than this méihuā, Mama.

I dig my nails into my leg so hard that I wonder if it'll bruise tomorrow, and the pain releases me from my unwanted reverie. Soon, it'll be time to focus on Ella, but not yet. I can't let the garden swallow me whole like it swallowed up my baby girl, leaving nothing but insubstantial memories.

When I reach the spot where I saw the figure, there's nothing but dashed hopes and empty air waiting for me.

But I'm not about to give up.

"Ella?" I call out softly. The acoustics of the empty garden carry my voice farther than expected. "Ella? It's Mama. I miss you, baby girl."

I stop to listen, hearing only the vibrato of insects and patter of small animals trudging through the garden foliage. As I resume walking, I call for Ella in intervals until I reach the pavilion where Anton and I got engaged. I stand under the peaked roof, clutching one of the poles as the weight of loss hits me.

I've heard of couples growing apart after their child died, but Anton and I were one of those annoyingly perfect *goals* couples. When he asked me to marry him, I didn't hesitate for even a millisecond. Smugly, I thought nothing could ever tear us apart.

No one told me I wasn't just losing Ella; I was losing Anton, too.

I turn and kick the hapless rail enclosing the pavilion, and my toe protests. The pain is refreshing as I push away thoughts of my estranged husband. I can't think about him. Not here, not today, not right now.

I sit on the bench with my eyes closed, leaning back against the railing, and giving myself permission to do the one thing that helps almost as much as it hurts. I think about Ella.

Ella, with her squishy eyes, tiny fingers, and matted brown hair falling asleep against my chest after nursing. Ella, pointing and making excited toddler noises when she sees the fox-shaped cake I baked for her second birthday. Ella, the first time she ran too fast and tripped on the sidewalk, skinning her knee.

Something tickles my hair. I reach up to swipe away whatever insect has landed on me. Instead, my fingers grasp soft petals, closing around what appears to be a flower in full bloom. I pull it down to take a look as a familiar fragrance fills the pavilion.

It's a *méihuā*, far out of season in August.

And it's exactly like the one Ella plucked for me last year.

I stare at the impossible blossom. Watch as it crumples, petals turning brown, before it decays into a slimy mess before my eyes.

What. The. Fuck?

"Ella?" I call out, scrambling to my feet.

No response.

I swivel my head from side to side, trying to make out her tiny shape, but the garden is filled with shadows. I wipe the dark, cold slime onto my jeans as I start walking, calling Ella's name, knowing I sound frantic, but unable to stop the desperation from tumbling out.

"Ella? Ella, baby, come back. I can't live without you. Mama doesn't want to live without you. Please please *please please please...*"

Tears fall, obscuring my vision, but I can't stop moving, can't stop desperately seeking my baby.

Mama?

Her voice calls from up ahead and I run forward, stumbling on an errant vine and falling onto a bed of delicate purplish buds that spill over the ground, darkness casting them the color of a bruise. Ignoring the pain that bursts through my hands and knees, I push to my feet and keep running.

Mama? Help!

My baby is out there. Ella is out there. She needs me, she's here...

In the distance, I hear the squelch of soggy footsteps, like someone stepping out of a creek into the mud. I turn toward the sound, heart racing as the shadow of something shifts near the water's edge. A mix between dread and anticipation slithers up my spine as I head for the pond.

As I cut across the courtyard, the sound of splashing draws my attention. Too loud for the tame koi in this pond. I pick up the pace, heart beating like drums. That almost sounded like...

... someone falling in.

"Ella!" I sprint toward the stone footbridge. Someone is kneeling by the shore, their arms in the water. I can't make out any features, just a hunched shape like darkness manifest, and I'm plunged back into memory...

Ella, in the little red qípáo that I thought would be adorable to dress her in for Ghost Day, lying face down in the pond, unmoving in the murky waters...

... their head lifts as I approach, and as the light from nearby lotus lanterns hits their face, all I see is two empty eye sockets, stringy red tendon trailing out from one, like someone gouged out what used to be there... and a row of rotted teeth that twists upward into a feral grin. It shoves down hard on the thing in the water, the tiny person struggling against an inhuman force, the face-down girl with two little braided buns sticking straight up...

I scream, and all of the lanterns snuff out.

CHAPTER 4

I lunge forward, screaming as I fumble to pry the thing off my little girl—the thing that's *drowning her*—but my eyes haven't adjusted to the change in lighting and I can't see anything at all, as if the moon itself had vanished.

Wet, bony hands shove me backward with shockingly strong force. The back of my head hits one of the decorative rocks with a crack, and pain overpowers everything. Involuntary tears stream down my face as I grit my teeth and use my elbows for leverage to push myself back up. I've failed her once before; I won't fail Ella again.

Stumbling to my feet, I summon my adrenaline and lunge for the thing, wrestling it away from my Ella. With one hand, I manage to grasp its surprisingly warm, soft skin and dig my nails in. I reach back the other fist and land a punch, feeling my knuckles hit bone.

It lets out a startlingly human screech and starts shouting. Finally, my brain registers that it's saying my name; then I recognize the voice.

"Sarah?"

"Yes! What the fuck, Jodi?"

Heart pounding, I fall back into a sitting position on the grass, reaching back and gingerly touching my head wound as my eyes slowly adjust. Sarah grimaces, pulling down her collar to reveal a blooming dark spot on her shoulder bone, surrounded by tiny, demilune indents. Her dark brown eyes stare into mine, the look of incredulity unmistakable.

"I'm... I'm sorry. Something was drowning her." My voice comes out a croak. My heart is still sprinting, mind stuck looping the image of the thing shoving down my baby girl. Holding her under the water...

"Jodi!" Sarah lets out a frustrated sound, running her fingers through her hair and pulling the strands back so tight I can see bits of her scalp. She squeezes her eyes shut and sighs, long and drawn-out. When she speaks again, it's in the soft, cautious tones everyone used at Ella's funeral. "Look. There's no one here but us."

I turn toward the spot where my little girl had been, unable to reconcile the calm waters and glowing lanterns with the images fixed in my mind. Sarah's right. There's no creature. No blood. No sign of struggle at all.

No Ella.

I let out a choked sob as Sarah wraps me in her arms. Guilt and self-loathing fill in the empty spaces between us as my tears soak into the spot where I hit her.

"I'm sorry."

"I know."

"I miss her so much," I whisper.

"I know," she repeats, stroking my hair. The touch of her soft fingers and the soothing, rhythmic motion sends waves of relief through me. I burrow my head further into her knit sweater as tears continue to leak out.

Sarah stops suddenly, drawing away from me. Hurt, I sit back. She frowns, looking at her fingertips.

They're covered in blood.

"Jodi, you have a head wound."

"Yeah... I hit the rock when it shoved me... when I fell backwards."

Sarah stands up. "This is serious! We need to get you medical attention now." She bites her lip, staring down at me. "You might be hallucinating because of a head injury."

"No!" My voice comes out angrier than I intended, as I get to my feet. "You have the order wrong. I saw that *thing* first, then it shoved me against the rock. Sarah, I'm not seeing things. It was trying to hurt her!"

"You can't hurt someone who's already dead!"

48

For a moment, we stare at each other.

Sarah is the first to look down. "I... shouldn't have said it that way. This place is giving me the creeps. I'm sorry, Jodi. I know the first anniversary is hard."

Anniversary. I suddenly hate that word with a passion. It used to mean weekend getaways and candle-lit dinners with Anton. Now, it's a tainted word. Now, everything seems to spell Ella.

"You don't know that ghosts can't be hurt." I know I sound unreasonably stubborn, but I worry my lip and don't take the words back.

I stare down at the pond, at the spot where *it* was, but it's peaceful now. Orange koi swim in unison and light reflects off the pond's gentle ripples, like a big fucking betrayal.

"Maybe we should go home. Or take you to the E.R." Sarah's voice is too even, unnaturally still against the swirling night air.

"No! We can't leave." I try to calm my tone, afraid Sarah won't take me seriously unless I sound more rational. "I... want to stick around for a few more minutes. Just in case." The warmth of humiliation fills my cheeks.

Sarah takes a deep breath. "Okay, we'll stick to the plan. But if you start having any concussion symptoms, I'm taking you straight to the hospital."

I nod, relief pouring through me. She's not leaving me alone.

"I won't let you walk around with your head bleeding, though," she adds.

"We didn't exactly bring a first aid kit."

Sarah's eyes light up. "First aid kit! Maybe there's one in the bathroom."

I can tell she isn't going to let this go, so I let her drag me to the restroom, where she cleans and binds my wound as well as she can, given that neither of us has any idea what we're doing. Each time she dabs my cut with rubbing alcohol, it's like a hornet's barb piercing the tender back of my head.

As the adrenaline fades, I start to wonder.

What if Sarah's right? The garden is full of strange sounds. Maybe the wind carried with it whispers of nocturnal creatures conferring with one another. Maybe I just wanted to hear Ella.

Maybe the thing I saw was an invention of my imagination.

I don't know what to think anymore. The events of the night combine with the fatigue that always follows reminiscences of Ella, and I feel a bone-weary exhaustion shudder through my body.

We put the first aid kit away and walk back down the hallway to the teahouse. As we approach, the rank odor of damp mold and something decaying wafts toward us.

"What is *that?*" Sarah pinches her nostrils.

"You smell it too? I was half-hoping that smell was some kind of weird, sensory hallucination."

"Of course, I smell it. That's *rank*."

"Maybe it's the Spitting Ghost," I say.

"Oh my god, don't joke about that," Sarah says, shuddering. "That story was disgusting."

"Your favorite movie is *The Ring*, but some story about an old lady that spits gross water scares you?"

"It doesn't *scare* me, it's just gross. Shut up!"

I smirk but cover my nose with my sleeve as the odor grows stronger.

"What the fuck?" Sarah says, picking up one of the containers of food. She pops open the lid and a powerful stench wafts free, turning my stomach. I cover my mouth to keep from barfing. I back away, but Sarah peeks inside, nose wrinkled.

At a loss, I say the first thing that comes to mind. "Breathing that in probably isn't good for Baby Henry."

Sarah ignores me, staring at the food she'd lovingly cooked for our offerings. "It's rotted through." Incredulity makes her voice rise. "That's impossible. I made everything fresh this morning." She clutches the Tupperware so hard her knuckles turn white.

Afraid she'll work herself up enough to want to leave, I pry the container out of her hands and peek inside. The gelatinous pink rice cakes are covered in black fuzz, so far gone that chunks are missing, as if the mold was so voracious that it ate parts of them. The rice cakes are moving.

"Oh, gross!" I snap the lid shut on the mealy, wriggling maggots, shoving the Tupperware so hard it skates across the floor, landing near the sink. We *ate* those rice cakes. My stomach crawls as I think about tiny eggs hatching inside me, maggots pouring into my belly. The thin hairs on my arm prickle like they're crawling all over me. I brush them again and again, but the feeling won't go away.

Sarah stands up. "I'm going to take that container to the outside trash... and then brew us some tea."

I stare at her, surprised by her calm. But I'm relieved that she hasn't brought up going home again. She picks up the Tupperware and heads outside.

When I'm sure Sarah's out of earshot, I whisper. "Ella?"

There's no response, but she has to be here, somewhere, her spirit lost in the garden where she died. She asked me for help before *it* tried to drown her.

"Ella? Did that *thing* make the rice cakes mold? Ella, Mama will help you, whatever you need. Tell me what to do. Please, baby girl."

It's a while before footsteps announce Sarah's return. I whisper for Ella one more time before Sarah strides through the door.

"Did you get lost?" I ask.

"Sorta." She wrinkles her nose. "I didn't want that container anywhere near us, so I found a trash can that was far off. Got a bit turned around on my way back."

"Ah... I realized I should've started heating up the water."

"It's fine," Sarah says, grabbing a kettle and filling it. Her voice is still calm and flat, and I wonder what's going through her mind.

I lean against the wall, instantly realizing my mistake as my head wound throbs in response. Sarah brews the tea and pours out two cups. It's warm in my hands as I blow absently, watching wisps of steam waft up from the boiling liquid. I glance down, wondering if it's ready to drink, and see something inside. Leaves from the tea?

I lean down for a closer look, making out the shape of a tiny, perfectly formed *méihuā* resting at the bottom of my teacup. Startled, I blink, and the flower is gone.

Ella?

Does she want me to drink it? I take a long sip. The tea is still slightly too warm. It singes my tongue and throat, but I take another sip, thinking of Ella. I drink the whole cup, eyelids fluttering closed even as I set it down, drifting off to sleep where I sit.

***

It's nighttime and I'm at the Ghost Garden, standing in the moon gate.

"Mama! You came!" Ella runs up to me, cheeks dimpling as she grins wide, putting her tiny hand in mine. I squeeze her hand as tears spill from my eyes, though I'm not sure why. Ella and I spend every day together and we've visited this place several times; why should today feel different? Yet the feeling of her hand in mine feels precious, like it could slip away at any moment. I shake away the silly thought as Ella pulls me forward.

"Mama, we have to hide!" She giggles as she pulls me behind the tree.

"Wait, Ella! Why?" I try to stop her, but she's surprisingly strong for a four-year-old. Four? Or is she three? How could I forget my daughter's age? Where are we going?

"Mama, come *on*," she says, pulling harder, and I give in. My thoughts feel hazy, and it's easier not to fight. Besides, the worst thing that'll happen is I'll get a little extra cardio.

She pulls us behind a huge tree, branches spread like a sea fan. There are leaves everywhere forming a thick, verdant layer that's nearly solid; pockmarks of moonlight shine through in the few spots where the leaves are less dense.

"Ella?"

Somberly, she raises a finger to her lips. I want to ask her why we're being quiet, but she looks so serious that the words die on my tongue.

Muffled, dragging footsteps sound from the other side of the bush; slow and squelching, like feet trawling through the mud. My nose wrinkles as I breathe in the scent of something moldy and rotting. My instincts scream at me to pick up Ella and run. But Ella's grip tightens in mine, so hard that pain shoots through my hand, keeping me in place.

As the steps near, most of the light vanishes, leaving us shrouded in darkness. I look at Ella, the whites of her eyeballs somehow still visible as she stares at the bush like she knows what's on the other side. It reminds me of the night she insisted someone was tapping at her window. It turned out to be a branch, half torn from the tree during a windstorm, but Ella wasn't convinced. She was so sure that someone was coming to steal her away.

She looks more afraid now than she did then.

I have the distinct impression of something turning toward us as the stench of foul breath mixed with rotting meat nearly makes me gag aloud. I bite my tongue, determined not to let Ella down.

The thing turns and shuffles away with its strange, dragging step. Minutes pass before Ella or I move an inch. Finally, she turns to me. She opens her mouth and I kneel down so she can whisper in my ear.

"Mama, you have to find the truth."

"Ella, what are you talking about? What *is* that thing?"

"Mama." She's so scared she's blubbering, and I pull her to me for a hug, but she steps away from me. Her voice begins slurring, and she steps back again.

"Tell... the... truth."

"The truth about what? Ella, baby?"

She keeps stepping back, growing smaller as the distance between us widens, and I try to lunge forward, but my feet are rooted to the ground. "Ella!"

Suddenly, Ella snarls. "You left me! She says she's my new mama." Ella steps back, a splash of water sounding and then the thump of a tiny body falling into the pond. I scream as the garden fades. Before I'm thrown back into consciousness, I hear one last thing. A voice, raspy and ancient, like something dug up from a grave.

Ràng wǒ jìn lái.

I wake to the sound of shattering glass.

CHAPTER 5

M y eyes snap open. I must have somehow fallen asleep while sitting up. Adrenaline pumps through my veins as I look around. The inflections were slightly strange, but the gravelly voice still lingers in my mind.

Ràng wǒ jìn lái.

Let me in.

What the fuck is going on?

Glass shatters loudly from down the hall again and I spin toward the sound. It takes a minute to clear enough dream fog and panic away to realize that Sarah isn't next to me anymore. My mind conjures the image of Sarah splayed out on the floor, bleeding, while a masked intruder stabs her repeatedly with a glass shard.

I tell myself she probably went to the bathroom and ran into something by accident, wincing as the sound of more glass breaking travels up the hallway. My brain still feels foggy, but I force myself into action, looking around for a weapon—just in case. My eyes land on a block of Shun knives.

Perfect.

I reach for the biggest looking knife, curling my fingers around the grip of a cleaver. My hand hurts as I clench it and I inspect my skin briefly, noticing red streaks, the size of a three-year-old's fingers.

Ella was trying to tell me something.

No. Help Sarah first, then worry about the dream.

I grab the knife and run toward the exhibit hall. Momentum carries me forward and before I can think about it, I'm rushing in brandishing a giant butcher's knife, ready to fight off the intruder...

... just as Sarah, using both arms to wield a cast-iron pan, brings it down on one of the display cases, shattering it to pieces.

I flinch, taking an involuntary step back as glass shards fly everywhere, but Sarah doesn't seem to notice. She steps toward another display case, lifting the pan again, and my mouth drops open as I realize she's not wearing shoes.

Her once-lavender, skull print ankle socks are soaked dark red.

"Sarah!" I yell.

She turns to me, and the pupils of her eyes are entirely white.

She turns her head back to her task and continues smashing up the displays.

I'm torn between the desire to get as far away as possible from Sarah's vacant stare and bloodied feet... and the part of me that's cycling through every time Sarah was there for me when no one else was.

Fuck it.

I set down the knife and walk toward Sarah, grateful I fell asleep without removing my shoes. I kick away the particularly large glass shards; some of them look long enough to pierce the soles of my sneakers. I brace myself, waiting for Sarah to turn around and smash my brains in with her cast-iron pan, but she's focused on her task.

"Sarah!" I shake her. She elbows me in return, readying to strike again. "Sarah, snap out of it!" I push her arms right as she's smashing down. She stumbles and the pan catches the corner of the display case. I wince as it cracks. I reach out and try to yank away the pan without hurting her or her protruding belly. She recovers fast and knees me hard, in the stomach. I gasp as pain shoots through me.

It's obvious that what I'm doing isn't reaching her.

I don't think I can stop her from hurting me or injuring herself, so I try a new tactic.

"You're Sarah Li-Jing Xu. You're twenty-seven, wife to Ken Xu and mother to Sean Xu. You have a little baby boy named Henry on the way soon, and he needs you." My voice chokes when I mention Henry, but I clear my throat and continue. "You're my best friend, and I'm so fucking lucky that I met you. Without you, I don't know if I would have survived an entire year without my Ella." At that, a sob escapes. I wipe it away angrily, then realize that Sarah has stopped moving. She's still gripping the pan tight, not looking at me, but she's not smashing anything up. I'm getting through to her. Hurriedly, I continue, words coming out so fast they squish together like drunken babble.

"You saved me. Planning and executing our adventures together gives me something to look forward to. Something more than the pain and dread I wake to each morning when I realize I'm living in a world where my baby no longer exists. You never judge me for the form my grief takes, you never push me to talk about her unless I want to, and you never ask for more than I have to give that day. You're the only person in the world who understands me anymore." I can't help the tears streaming down my face now.

Strong arms wrap around me. I can feel the hard metal shape of the pan against my back, and I flinch back as Sarah's stomach bumps into mine, hitting the spot where she kneed me. But she doesn't choke me or bash in my brains. Sarah wraps me in a hug.

And then she curses, stepping back.

"Fuckety fuck fuck *fuck me that hurts!*"

Desperate, relieved laughter pours out of me in peals as I look into Sarah's very normal, brown pupils. She reaches out instinctively toward something to hold her up, to take the weight off her bloody feet. I hold her up with all of my strength before she can put her hand on the sharp, jagged edge of a broken display case.

"What happened?" Sarah is breathless, wincing with the pain.

"Careful," I say. "Here, I'll carry you. Get on my back."

"Dude, my pregnant ass would squish you in two seconds flat." Her grip on my shoulder tightens. "Oh fuck. Oh my god. What have I done? Henry!" Her eyes fill with panic.

"Sarah!" I muster all the authority I can, and she turns to me with desperate eyes. "I didn't see any cuts on your stomach, but we'll make sure the baby is okay as soon as we get away from the broken glass."

"Okay. Yeah, okay. Okay."

I can feel her muscles tense with each painful movement as she lets me lead her out of the exhibit hall, one careful step at a time.

"I need to throw up," she whispers.

I nod, and together, we hobble over to the bathroom. True to her word, she heaves into the toilet as I do everything I can to hold her up and keep her long, shiny black hair back. It glistens with sweat, clinging to her forehead.

When she's done, I flush the toilet for her and get ready to help her back to the teahouse.

"I... can't walk again yet, Jodi. It hurts so much. Let's please check on the baby here."

"Okay. I'll help you onto the seat." I put down the toilet lid and help her sit. Thanks to her sweater, most of the glass shards didn't pierce her skin. I help her remove it carefully, setting it aside. There are a few cuts, and I hesitate, thinking of the first aid kit she used earlier on my head injury.

"Henry first," she says.

I nod, touching the hem of her shirt.

"May I?" I ask, and she nods.

I lift the shirt up over her head and run my hands along the taut skin of her swollen belly. There's a vertical line of dark brown spots down the middle of her stomach, splitting it into halves. I have a matching line on my own abdomen from when I was carrying Ella. It was one of those surprising pregnancy symptoms that often stays forever, like stretch marks and feet that go up a half size.

Sarah's skin is warm and damp against my fingers, and I'm relieved to feel a powerful kick.

"I think Henry's okay," I say, smiling.

She lets out a sigh of relief. "I felt him kick, but... I wanted to be sure it wasn't just me, hoping," she admits, as I gently tug the fabric back over her skin.

"He's got strong legs, like his mom."

I mean to make light of what happened, but Sarah frowns. "I... kicked you, didn't I. I'm sorry."

"Sarah, I..." I don't know what to say. *You seemed possessed?* I would flip shit if someone told me that. And truth or not, she probably does need to chill a bit, for her baby's sake if not for her own. She's in the third trimester, and a lot can go wrong in the home stretch.

She gulps, looking down. "I don't know why I did it. It's like... something told me. Well, that's not right. It wasn't a voice, more an instinct guiding me. I think it started with the rice cake." She presses her lips together. "Whatever-it-was led me to a plant in the garden and... made me pluck a few leaves to put in your tea."

"What?" I draw back in shock, and my back clatters against the stall door.

"Oh, not to poison you or anything," she says, as if that's supposed to reassure me.

"Then... why?"

"To make you fall asleep." She shakes her head. "That sounds bad. But... it seemed like a good idea. I don't know why. Then, once you fell asleep, it seemed like a good idea to pick up the pan and bring it to the main room. You saw the rest." She bites her lip. "You... believe me, right?"

"Yeah. Oh, yeah I definitely believe you, Sarah." I'm startled to realize that's what she was nervous about. "Um... your eyes were white, like you were possessed or something."

"Oh god," she says, hugging herself. "Jodi... I want to go home."

The situation is so strange that I have a sudden, inappropriate urge to make a joke about who the wimp is now. But I look into the big doe-eyes of my best friend. The bravest person I know is scared out of her mind. And I swallow the words along with my protests. She deserves to get out of whatever is going on.

I'll make sure Sarah gets out and I'll call Ken to pick her up at the gate.

Then I'll come back in to find Ella.

Sarah won't like it, but she doesn't have to know yet. It's my choice.

"Okay," I tell her, and her entire body slumps in relief.

She nods. "Thank you."

The logistics get a bit complicated as we sort out the best plan of escape. I offer to help her out first, then come back for the stuff, but she doesn't like the idea of me being alone in the garden. Unfortunately, she's the exercise fanatic, not me, and I barely have enough muscle to carry her out without all the extra stuff. I could bring the things out first, but then she would be alone in the garden.

I sigh in frustration. "Let's just leave the stuff. It's not ideal, but I can sneak back in at dawn and grab it." I wince. "I'll try to sweep up the glass a bit too."

She gives me a guilty look. "Honestly, at this point I don't even mind owning up to the damage. What I did to this place was horrible." She shakes her head. "But we can still leave you out of it."

"Sarah…"

"Don't argue with me! Let's get all traces of you out of here. I don't like the idea of you coming back in at dawn. What if someone who works here shows up at five or something?"

"The garden doesn't open until ten."

"Yeah, but I saw the bakery display and the "made from scratch" signs in the kitchen. Someone must come in to start baking early in the morning."

I sigh. "Well, what do *you* think we should do, then?"

She sighs too. "Goddamned feet." Then her face lights up. "Oh, I'm an idiot. We have a wheelchair!"

"We?" I lift her chin, looking into her eyes. What if she's still being possessed by… the garden, or the ghost of the garden or something?

Sarah rolls her very normal-looking eyes. "Give me a chance to finish. At my workplace, we have a wheelchair in case anyone needs it. I was thinking the garden might have the same."

"Oh yeah, good idea! But... do you want me to leave you alone while I go look for it?" I frown.

"No," Sarah says quickly, a lingering touch of panic in her voice. "It would have to be at the front somewhere, right? Or if they have an employee only area or something. I can walk over with your help. Whatever was guiding me wanted you asleep, probably to split us up. I don't think either of us should be alone."

"Okay," I say. "But what if there isn't a wheelchair?"

"Then we'll be a little closer to the front gate," she says. "You're right about the stuff. We'll figure out how to get out and worry about the rest later."

It takes ages for us to make it to the front. I can tell Sarah is trying to keep from crying out, but several small whimpers escape anyway. Eventually, we reach our destination. To our mutual relief, there's a rickety old wheelchair in the front closet. Carefully, I help Sarah lower herself into the seat. She sags in relief.

"Want me to push the chair for you, or would you rather wheel it yourself?"

"Push me, please. I'm so fucking exhausted," Sarah says.

"You got it."

After a quick debate, we decide to go back for our stuff, since it'll be way easier to haul everything with us now that we have the wheelchair. I can tell Sarah's relieved when we have everything packed up and ready to go. She places both hands on her belly as she leans back into the chair, and I bite my lip, looking straight ahead. Trying not to let the seething jealousy creep out.

Sarah's my best friend. I want her to be happy. She lost a child too. Her baby boy doesn't take anything away from me.

In my mind, I repeat the words to myself as we set off into the garden. The zig-zag path is just wide enough for the wheelchair and I maneuver carefully. My balance is thrown off by my wearing both our backpacks. There's one sleeping bag hanging off each handle of the wheelchair, and the tightly rolled bags knock against the sides of the pavilion as we cross through it.

It's a bumpy ride, but Sarah doesn't talk or complain, letting me keep my focus on avoiding running into things in the dark. The wooden walkway turns into the stone path and we near a white wall, ahead.

When we're almost at the moon gate, Sarah sits up so suddenly that I stop.

"What's wrong?" I ask her. Did the baby stop kicking for too long? Is she bleeding?

She's so tense that my own muscles tense in response.

Sarah shakes her head, staring into the distance. "This isn't right."

I follow her gaze past the moon gate, toward…

… what should be the stone-tiled entryway.

Instead, the pathway leads to a pavilion and another grand building, an exact reflection of the path we came from. I look backwards to confirm the museum is still there.

It is. It's behind us and ahead of us.

My heart pounds as I begin walking again, pushing Sarah's wheelchair forward.

"What are you doing?" she asks.

"I… we have to get to the front gate."

"It's gone!"

"It can't be gone! That's impossible!"

She looks back at me and I see my own terror reflected in her face. "What do we do?"

"I don't know. Let's keep going. Maybe… we should both close our eyes when we cross through the gate? I don't know! Maybe it's a mirage? Or something?"

"Okay." Sarah sounds equally unconvinced, but what choice do we have?

When we reach the gate, we both close our eyes as we cross the threshold, waiting a count of ten before opening them again.

It's like we've just entered the garden. The pavilion and museum loom up ahead.

"Oh my god," Sarah says, fear entering her voice. "What do we do? Jodi what do we do we're trapped here oh my god we're going to die here..."

"Sarah, stop! I think there's a back gate. We can try that path."

Sarah snaps her lips shut, biting back the panicked words that I'm certain are desperate to escape. She nods, and by unspoken mutual agreement, we continue in silence. There's nothing to be gained by talking about it; all our words serve to do is confirm that the impossibility we're in is really happening.

I take the path that should lead to the other exit. My body relaxes marginally when I see the back gate ahead.

We keep going until my arms and legs have grown so tired that I want to lay down and sleep in the field, letting the ground swallow me up whole.

We keep going, long past the point where it becomes clear that the wall and the tantalizing back gate aren't getting any closer.

We keep going until finally, Sarah reaches back and puts her hand on mine, whispering defeated words. "There's no point."

I shake my head, even though she can't see me, exhaustion ringing through my bones.

"We'll never reach either gate," she says.

I stop, making sure the brake is on Sarah's wheelchair before coming around to face her. I know what she'll say next but knowing doesn't make it any easier to hear.

"Jodi, we can't escape. The garden won't let us leave."

As her words rush into the air, the leaves around us begin to wither and rot. Flower petals blacken and melt into dark slime, which seeps into the ground. Water rises up to cover the ground and Sarah squeaks as we begin sinking into the thick mud. Everything molds and decays before our very eyes, as if the garden speaks its own language. It doesn't need human words to tell me what it's saying.

You're trapped here.

CHAPTER 6

Afraid we'll end up sucked into a sinkhole, I release the brake on the wheelchair and start wheeling Sarah through the sludge. I concentrate on moving, trying to ignore the garden withering around us. If I stare for too long, I'm pretty sure I'll start screaming and never stop.

My sneakers sink in with each muddy step.

"What do we do?" Sarah's fear compounds my own, and I put everything I have into concentrating.

Think. Think. Think, damnit!

"Oh! Sarah, your phone. Do you have your phone? We can call someone!"

She shakes her head. "I... think I smashed it up earlier."

"Fuck. Okay. Um... the ghost. It tried to tell me something." My words are a jumbled, incoherent mess, but I stumble through, mind racing from thought to thought.

"The ghost talked to you?" Sarah sounds even more afraid now.

"No, no. Well, yes. But Ella is the one who told me. The ghost—Ella calls it the scary lady—wants something. It..." *...says she's my new mama!* "...wants the truth, or something. It wants us to tell the truth!"

"The truth about what?"

"I don't know. But we have to find the truth!"

"That's so vague!" Sarah's voice rises with mine. She taps her fingers against the wheelchair, the noise making it hard to concentrate. I wish she would *stop.*

"I know. But Sarah... I don't think we're getting out of here unless we figure out."

Her breaths come faster now, quick and shallow. "Okay, think. Let's be rational."

A low, rumbling laugh comes from my throat, sounding warped and wrong. "Rational? There's nothing fucking *rational* about this! We're trapped in a fucking maze we can't escape, and a ghost is trying to steal my daughter!"

"What?"

"She wants Ella." I bite my lip. "I told you before she was trying to drown Ella. Probably so she'd stay truly dead forever. And Ella said the ghost says she's Ella's new mom."

"What the fuck? So, it's like... a child-stealing ghost?"

"I guess? I have no idea!"

"No, no, this is good," Sarah says, voice hiccupping as her wheelchair hits a half-rotten root. The plants are no longer confined by human-defined boundaries. Slimy ferns and thorny vines creep onto the path. "Maybe it—or *she*, I guess—is one of the ghosts from the garden. She has to be, right? What if... god, this sounds dumb, but I mean... some supernatural shit is going down here so bear with me... what if one of the artifacts actually did come tethered to a ghost?"

"You always want everything to be in neat little boxes."

"Oh my god, Jodi, stop being antagonistic. This could get us out of here, okay?"

I take a deep breath. Sarah's right. It's not like I have any better ideas. "Okay. Where do you want to start?"

"The exhibits, I think."

When I pushed Sarah toward the back gate, it felt like we'd been walking for an eternity. I expected to exhaust myself on the trip back, but in no time at all, we're already at the museum. The incongruity makes me shiver almost as much as seeing black mold covering the bushes we pass. Almost as much as the crimson stains on the rocks and the murky water that appears impossibly deep at a glance.

Almost as much as the rising scent of death and decay wafting from the garden.

My stomach churns at the odor and I try not to think about the maggots from earlier.

Despite the strangeness of the rotting garden, I had expected the museum to remain exactly the same. But as we approach, I realize the wood is cracked, the lattices half gone, the remaining pieces full of tiny holes, like a swarm of termites had come through for a buffet. I reach out to push open the door, immediately regretting using my bare hands as the soggy board presses in at my touch.

"It didn't even rain," I say, as if that were the most incredible thing that had happened tonight.

"I don't think we should stay in here for long," Sarah says, staring at a spot where the door frame has splintered. "Whatever's happening to the garden is creepy as fuck, but... this building looks ready to collapse at any moment." She looks down. "Or sink into the mud."

"Maybe we should grab the audio guides and listen to the stories outside." I shiver, thinking about us both listening to ghost stories while a real ghost sneaks up on us and... "One of us could listen while the other acts as a lookout?"

"Sure. I'll listen to the headset since you have to navigate."

I move to step inside, leaving Sarah outside. We'll only be a few feet from one another and within viewing distance.

Sarah grabs my arm, stopping me. "What if crossing a threshold separates us?"

"Alright, we'll go together." I wheel Sarah inside and the floorboards groan dangerously. "Let's just make it quick."

Inside, I pull an audio guide off the stand and hand it to Sarah.

"Don't let anything jump me, okay?" Her mouth quirks into a half-grin and I snort as she jams the headset on. She starts listening to ghost stories as I angle the wheelchair back around.

In the corners of my vision, something flickers, and I turn my head.

The figure is mostly hidden by the darkness, but I catch the shape of a small face, two little buns atop its head. The figure lifts a finger to their lips. *Shhh…*

Ella!

I run toward her, but she disappears around a corner. Desperate, I follow her, rounding the bend to a tight stairwell and a rickety old ramp. No Ella.

"Jodi? Jodi!" Sarah calls out, followed by the fumble of metal and squeak of wheels on old floorboards.

I run past the "Employees Only" sign, leaping up the stairwell in search of my baby girl. "Ella!"

But there's nothing. No patter of footsteps, no *Mama!*

"Jodi! Where are you?" Sarah's voice sounds frenzied, and guilt settles over me. She asked me not to leave her behind.

I run back down, each stair shaking uneasily with my steps.

"Sorry."

"What the fuck? I thought we weren't separating?"

"I know, I'm sorry. I saw Ella."

Sarah's eyes widen. "What…"

"I think she wants us to look upstairs."

"What? Why? I thought we were going back outside! What's upstairs?" Sarah's voice rises.

"The employee-only section is up there. They might have more information on the ghosts and exhibits, or something else that would help us figure out what's going on. You can listen while I look around."

Sarah shakes her head vehemently. "I don't think we should go there."

"But…"

"Every second we stay in this building is a second we might cause a cave-in. We shouldn't be arguing right now! I mean, look how much the floors are creaking down here. And I… have a bad feeling."

"I know." It *is* a terrible idea. "But I have to trust Ella. She wouldn't lead us into danger."

"Even if you really saw her, she's *three*."

"Oh my god, you still don't believe something supernatural is going on? Sarah, what the hell will it take, if all of this—" I gesture around us "—doesn't convince you?"

Sarah lets out a frustrated noise. "Goddamnit, Jodi, it's not that. And we're wasting time!"

"Yeah, time we could spend figuring out what Ella wants us to see. What if the *truth* we need to find is up in that office and we spend so long arguing that the building collapses and then we're trapped here forever?"

We glare at each other.

Finally, Sarah sighs, face melting into a worn-out expression that tells me I've won. For now. "Let's make it quick, okay?"

She jams her headset back on, turning up the volume as I start wheeling her up the ramp.

I wince at every sound of the building slowly falling apart with us inside. One board buckles as we cross it, and Sarah's face grows ashen. But we make it upstairs.

Viscous, black slime seeps down from a hole in the ceiling and several ink-black beetles skitter across our path. I cough as my lungs fill with the musty, pungent scent of mildew. Boxes and piles of papers are scattered everywhere, like someone left in the middle of sorting through files. The unruly mess is enough to block the wheelchair's path.

I tap Sarah and she pulls off her headphones.

"I think I should look through everything while you listen to the rest of the stories. We can't get the wheelchair through here," I say.

"No!" Sarah lifts herself up. "I can walk a little bit."

"Sarah, your feet are bloody messes."

"I'm fine. I want to help."

"Then I'll pass you some papers," I say.

She shakes her head. "We need to get this shit sorted out as quickly as possible. I want to go home, Jodi."

I stare at her and she stares back, her pupils their usual dark brown. As far as I can tell, she's not being possessed. I relent. "Okay." I lean down to lend her my strength.

"Holy fuck, that hurts!" She clenches her teeth so hard her eyes start watering.

Together, we step over piles of papers, boxes, and a few empty mugs, making it to the center of the room, where there's a small desk and chair. The seat creaks as she sits down, but it holds her weight.

I take in our surroundings with dismay. If we have to sort through every pile in here, we'll be dead long before we have the chance to figure out what the ghost wants.

"There!" Sarah says, pointing to a cabinet.

She found that fast. Too fast.

But as I look where she's pointing, I see that she didn't need supernatural guidance to realize this might be a good place to start. One of the filing cabinet drawers is labeled *Artifacts*.

The drawer has a keyhole above it and sure enough, when I try to pull it open, it's locked. When I turn to tell Sarah, she's holding something up with two fingers.

A tiny golden key.

"Try this," she says.

I don't move. "Where did you get that from?"

"From the desk drawer," she says. "It was right in here."

I keep staring at her.

"What?" She sounds annoyed. "We shouldn't be wasting time."

"I just... that was quick." My mind races. What if the ghost can possess her without giving a visible sign? Last time, she barely interacted with me while under the ghost's spell.

She's observant; she probably saw the key sitting atop the desk and connected the dots. I take it from Sarah's hand. "Thanks." But I don't turn my back to her as I try the lock. Just in case.

After a click, the drawer opens. Inside, there are section dividers denoting acquisition year. Each year contains folders labeled with the name of a ghost story. Perfect.

Spitting Ghost is the most recent, followed by *Ghost Mirror* and *Human Bench.* I skip past them, pulling files from the year the gardens were converted to Ghost Gardens. I hand half of them to Sarah and stand up, putting the rest on top of the file cabinet. I pick one up and flip through it. Everything related to the artifact acquisition is in here, including detailed notes scrawled in messy handwriting.

Tree Ghost Girl – Four travelers desperate for lodging agree to stay in the spare room at an inn. Room has one bed containing the innkeeper's dead daughter, covered by a paper shroud, awaiting burial. *(Full stop. DO NOT AGREE TO SLEEP IN A ROOM WITH A DEAD PERSON.)* They set up on the floor in one corner. Three fall asleep, but the other is too afraid. At night, he sees the dead girl lift up her shroud, creep out of bed, and walk over to where they're sleeping.

Traveler guy leaves his friends for dead *(kind of a dick move)*, using them as a distraction to run outside as the ghost murders his friends. She chases him out and he knocks on the door of a monastery, but they're afraid and lock him out while watching the scene from a window. *(LMAO at the monks shamelessly watching the drama unfold—hope they grabbed a bowl of whatever is ancient China's equivalent of popcorn.)*

The traveler runs behind a huge oak tree and the ghost tries to get at him, but he stays on the other side of the tree. Both grow tired. *(Meanwhile, the damn monks are watching the whole thing.)* At last, the ghost girl lunges, and he ducks. She gets stuck with her arms around the tree trunk, where they all find her in the morning.

The terrified traveler gets a travel allowance and a writ of certification from the local magistrate promising these events all truly happened, as witnessed by the local monks, so that he can go home safely without being accused of murdering his friends. *(Yay!)*

The artifact is supposedly a slice from the tree in the story. The seller swore authenticity, on his and all his ancestors' and children's lives. Dad checked and it's from a type of tree that grows in the area. Town elders say there used to be a monastery before it was destroyed during the cultural revolution. Dad also asked around town and confirmed that others had heard the same local ghost story, with about the right amount of variation for a tale passed down a century or two.

To-do: write the story in the ancient folklore style for museum viewing, consult Leo about the best way to preserve it, and add a glass case to the initial display order. Then get yourself a soy matcha latte because you've worked hard and they're fucking delicious.

Any other time, I'd want to find out which garden employee wrote this; they sound like fun. Sarah and I would totally befriend them; she's also a huge matcha fan. But I'm frustrated, unable to fathom any connection between the Tree Ghost Girl story and what's happening to us now.

After skimming the next few files, I end up setting them down and picking up the one I'm most interested in. I don't know if this is any help, but... it *is* the one tale that's tied to the family that owns the garden. Ning's file contains a little more information than the audiobook story, and I take note. I raise my eyebrows when I reach the details about Li and Ning's marriage. Her dowry included bedding, a tea set and chest of tea, bedroom slippers, a sewing kit, gold jewelry, her personal maid, two bags of gold, and a full wardrobe of outfits for every season.

"Ning's maid is considered part of her dowry. How fucked up is that?"

Sarah grimaces. "Super fucked up. Sadly, Europeans and Americans are far from the only ones to mess with slavery. Lovely cross-cultural commonality, isn't it?"

"Found anything?" I ask.

"I don't know. You said the ghost smelled awful, right? But the Spitting Ghost seems too recent to be behind all four years of Ghost Day mishaps. Maybe all ghosts smell awful?"

"Yeah. Or maybe there's something specifically tied to this day? After all, why is it happening on Ghost Day each year?"

"Because they're all ghosts and we're in a *ghost museum*?"

I let out a frustrated groan, setting down the file. I ask the air, only half-seriously. "Ella, can you help Mama understand? What truth does the ghost demand?"

She doesn't like liars, Mama. Tell the truth.

I jump and the floor creaks beneath me as I look around. But Ella isn't anywhere to be seen. I turn to Sarah whose eyes are wide. "I just heard Ella say..."

"...she doesn't like liars," Sarah repeats. "Tell the truth."

"Oh my god, you heard her too?"

"I did." She scans around the room. "Ella, can you tell us anything else?"

Silence.

"She keeps repeating the same thing," I say.

Sarah's nails tap against the file on her lap and she closes her eyes for a moment. Her next words are barely above a whisper. "What if the truth isn't directly about the ghost?"

I study her. "You mean like, it's about the garden somehow?"

"Maybe," she says, worrying her lip. "Or maybe it really is what Ella said. She doesn't like liars."

"Why, are you lying about something?" I joke.

She doesn't answer.

I feel the blood drain from my face. "Sarah?"

She starts biting her nails. "My family believes we've always had a strong connection to the ghost world," she says. "Something from ancient times."

I look at her, confused. "What does that have to do with the ghost?"

"Nothing," she says, shaking her head and sitting straight up. She opens the next file. "Let's keep looking."

I stare at her.

I really stare at her.

My friend, who didn't want me to come upstairs.

My friend, whose feet are cut up but who insisted on joining me anyway. On keeping an eye on my research.

My friend, who's afraid the ghost is coming after her because it doesn't like liars.

My friend, whom the ghost chose to possess.

My friend, who loves soy matcha lattes.

It can't be. She *can't* be.

I drop the files and start walking around the room. Refusing to believe it. Looking for whatever is in this room that she didn't want me to see. Hoping to be proven wrong.

"What are you doing?" Sarah leaps to her feet, hissing in pain as she grabs my shoulder, pulling me away from the wall behind the desk, and I know. I *know*.

I know what I'll see when my eyes land on the family portrait, hung up on the wall.

I know I'll recognize one of the faces smiling back at me.

Knowing doesn't hurt any less.

CHAPTER 7

"You're the daughter. *Your family owns the garden.*" My voice is too calm, too steady, concealing the rage simmering beneath the surface. I want Sarah to deny it, to roll her eyes and tell me that I'm an idiot. That there's no way she'd lie about something like this. And for what?

"I'm sorry." Sarah's voice is so small as she still leans on me, unable to stand on her own feet.

Pieces slot into place. That's why she wasn't worried about us being here overnight. That's why the door to the museum was left unlocked. That's why she knew she'd be able to take care of the damage downstairs, as long as no one found out I'd been here too. That's how she knew where the file cabinet key was. That's why she knew there would be a wheelchair in the front closet. That's why she didn't want me to come upstairs... in case I saw the photo.

A realization tickles my mind, but I don't want it. I don't want to know. I don't want to know I don't want to know I don't...

She doesn't like liars, Mama.

"You're the reason this is happening." My voice rises in volume as my anger builds. "The ghost is after *you*. *You're* the fucking liar." My voice breaks. "The only thing I don't understand is... *why?*"

My mind spins with thoughts, possibilities.

I don't want to know.

I need to know.

Sarah blinks, her breaths quick now, her voice barely a whisper. "I'm sorry, Jodi. I didn't mean for it to happen."

"For what to happen?" I know I should let her talk, but I can't help my rising rage.

"After... after last Ghost Day, I... tried to find you to make sure you were okay." She claps a hand over her mouth. "I mean... duh. You're not okay. Of course, you weren't okay. But I wanted to make things better, to lighten the load for you even if it was only a little bit." She looks up at me, a plea written in her eyes.

I don't speak.

Her words spill out faster, like tea pouring from a teapot, burning me. "You... were Facebook friends with my cousin, who works here. You mentioned a grief forum and I... found you on there."

She closes her eyes, leaning harder on my shoulder now. I tamp down the urge to fling her off me. I need to know.

"And Sean?"

She startles at the name, then a guilty expression crosses her face, and I clench my fist so hard it hurts.

"He's real," she whispers. "He is... was... my younger brother. The story I told you was true... except I'm his sister, not his mom."

I close my eyes as every lie she's told me pierces my heart.

"Please understand, Jodi, I never meant to hurt you." Sarah slides down to her knees, pressing her hands together in a begging motion. "I only wanted to check in, to see what I could do. But you're wry and funny and real, and you also loved morbid things. I fell... I think we were meant to become best friends. What we have is real. I *swear*."

I feel the sharp dig of my nails pressing into the skin of my leg. I take a long, deep breath before speaking again.

"And why," I say, voice colder than it's ever been, "did you feel guilty enough to seek me out in the first place?"

Sarah goes still. "Jodi..."

"Answer me."

"Okay, okay. You deserve to know." Sarah coughs. "Um... I really was gone for the first few years after my parents bought the garden. It was my idea to convert it and I helped with artifact acquisition and planning... anyway. I was finally back, and my parents wanted to introduce me to everyone, but I asked them to let me experience their big Ghost Day celebration without all the fuss of a million *āyís* wanting to know me." She bites her lip. "They let me be part of the catering staff."

My nails dig further into my flesh. Harder and harder.

"This little girl came up to me." Sarah's glance flicks upward. "Looking for her mom."

My teeth are clenched so tightly that I can feel the pressure as bone presses into bone.

"I told her I didn't know her mom, but I would help her look, right after I finished clearing the table." She closes her eyes, a teardrop running down her cheek. "We had just gotten a new batch of koi, and one had an almost-star-shaped marking on it. I was trying to keep her there, talking to her about the cool new fish in the garden. I told her that she and her mom should go look for the new fishy. But..." She bites her lip so hard a drop of blood spills out. She laps it up with her tongue before continuing. "... an elderly guest fell, and I got distracted trying to help him. By the time I got him settled, the little girl was gone. I figured her mom had come and taken her and went to clear the next table." Tears stream down her face now. "You know the rest."

My best friend looks pathetic, hunched down in front of me, crying her eyes out. The onslaught of emotions feels heavy and uncontrolled, like a tornado swirling through me. Rage and sadness and anger and one horrible, horrible, despicable emotion I hate myself for.

Envy.

Sarah has never lost a child.

Sarah is about to have her first kid.

Sarah was the last person to see Ella alive.

I help up my sniveling friend and she leans on me gratefully, looking at me with such sorrow, hope, and brokenness in her eyes that I can hardly stand it.

"I'm so sorry, Jodi. Please believe me. I swear I never meant to carry on deceiving you for so long. The more we got to know each other, the harder it became and... I didn't know how to tell you. I'm so, so sorry."

I look into my best friend's bloodshot, watery eyes, and I say the only thing I can think to say. "I forgive you."

Relief washes over her. "Ella was such a sweet girl, Jodi."

I let her finish talking. Then I shove her as hard as I can. She falls backwards, hitting the corner of a filing cabinet, and crumples to the floor.

***

Tears run down my face as I kneel besides Sarah. Is she breathing? Oh god, what if I've killed her?

What if I've killed her baby?

Oh my god, oh my god, oh my god... I put a hand over her mouth to see if she's still breathing.

A warm, faint puff of air brushes my fingertips.

I let out a huge sigh, leaning my cheek on her chest as I collapse onto her, sobbing, my tears soaking her sweater. She's not dead; I haven't killed her.

I still love her.

Almost as much as I hate her.

I sit up and look around, wondering if everything will go back to normal now that she's told her truth. But the room still feels strange, and I gag as a now-all-too-familiar scent fills the air.

Dead things.

I wipe away the tears and sit up, wondering what to do now. Should I drag Sarah somewhere? Leave her here?

A scream from downstairs makes the decision for me.

Mama! Help!

Ella's shrill cry pushes me to my feet in an instant. I don't spare a glance for Sarah as I run for the stairwell, nearly tripping in my haste to get downstairs.

"Ella? Baby girl, where are you?"

As I leap down the last few creaking steps, landing hard on both feet, I hear a sound from the exhibit hall. The pitter-patter of two tiny feet kicking against something.

Or someone.

Mama!

Ella's desperate cry is cut off by something muffled, like someone's covered her mouth.

"Ella!" I scream as I race down the corridor.

When I reach the exhibit hall, it's still a shock to see everything covered in shattered glass. The room is littered with half-broken display cases. Ning's scroll is torn, and the green embroidered slippers lay on the ground.

And in the huge, ornately carved Ghost Mirror framed by gilded fox spirits and celestial beings, I see the reflection of two figures.

A long-haired woman, sloughs of moist skin covering her skeleton, stands tall in a tattered Chinese dressing gown dripping with muddy water, eyes still empty but for the stringy red tendon draped from one socket. She looks like she climbed out of a wet, shallow grave long after her skin rotted into the soil and carrion birds reached in to pluck out her eyeballs. A primitive knife sticks from her chest and blood drips from the wound, staining her robe. She grins at me, jaws full of rotting, yellow teeth.

The long, skeletal fingers of her right hand cover Ella's mouth.

Her left hand wraps around Ella's throat.

I cry out, unable to keep calm and quiet in the face of Ella's visible fear. She kicks her little feet, trying to wriggle away to no effect. I remember how violently the ghost shoved me away when I tried to stop her from drowning my baby girl. Ella has no chance against her.

Sarah's truth didn't free us from this monster.

"No!" I scream. "You can't have her!" I run up to the mirror, pounding on the glass. Looking around, I catch sight of the pan Sarah abandoned and grab it, ready to smash the glass and free my baby.

The ghost grins wider. A low, throaty sound, almost a crow's caw, shakes the entire room as I lift the pan in the air.

If I shatter the mirror, I might trap Ella forever. Fuck! I don't know the rules to this ghost's game.

Trembling, I lower the pan. "Tell me what you want!" I demand. "I'll do anything to get my baby back. *Anything!*"

The ghost starts muttering. I recognize it as mostly Mandarin, albeit with an odd inflection to several words. Some kind of archaic dialect?

"Ella? What do I do, baby?" I look into my daughter's wide, terrified eyes. She mutters something, but it's muffled by the ghost's bony, rotting finger.

Ella's wide eyes flicker to the side and I follow her gaze to the glass cases Sarah destroyed.

The displays Sarah destroyed when the ghost was possessing her.

Oh, shit. The destruction wasn't random. The ghost told us exactly who she is.

I look around at what Sarah went after. The urn, the scroll, the slippers, and the painting.

All of them are part of Ning's display.

When I look back to the mirror, the scene has changed. Ella is bound to a small chair by vines, one stuffed in her mouth so she can't speak. She's crying and shaking her head, but the ghost ignores her. It stoops in front of her with a bucket of dark, murky pondwater, steam rising from the surface. I don't understand what it's doing, but Ella seems to. She cries and shakes her head, over and over.

"Ella? Baby, it'll be okay."

The ghost mutters incoherently as she dips Ella's feet in the water. Ella cries out, squirming away from the hissing water. The ghost pulls out a stained cloth and begins washing Ella's feet.

"Ning?" I try to grab the ghost's attention. She ignores me, muttering to herself as she pulls Ella's reddened feet out of the water and pulls the blade out of her chest.

"Ning!" Panicked words tumble out as I beg. "I don't know your truth. No one knows the true story. What happened to make you so angry? Please, let me help you. I swear I'll do anything if you leave Ella be."

The ghost continues muttering to herself, ignoring me. I cry out as the knife nears Ella's toes. I scream as she starts whittling away, until I realize she's cutting the ends off Ella's toenails. My mouth drops open as the ghost dips her hand into a small bowl of oil, rubbing it into Ella's foot.

Seriously, what the *fuck* is she doing?

That's when I realize I can understand what she's saying. She's still speaking in a dialect that's not quite Mandarin, but I can understand her perfectly.

Little girl, I'll be a good mama. Little girl, you won't suffer the way I did. Little girl, you'll be respectable. It'll only hurt a minute. Be still, little girl. Be still.

"Be still for what?" I press my hands and face up against the glass, as if I could reach through to the other side, but it stays solid, taunting me. Gently, the ghost uses a moth-eaten cloth to wipe down Ella's foot and dry her hands.

Mama! Tell her truth, Mama! Help! Even with the vines binding her mouth shut, I can hear Ella's cry as if she was screaming into my mind.

The ghost raises her head to look at me, a resigned smile replacing the feral grin from earlier, and then she cradles Ella's left foot in one hand.

With the other, she snaps Ella's toe.

CHAPTER 8

My scream echoes throughout the museum. I don't know who's screaming louder; me, or Ella, whose shrill cry fills my mind.

Mama Mama Mama you didn't stop her! It hurts! Mama, help!

"I'm sorry, baby." I'm a blubbering mess, watching in helpless horror as the ghost inspects Ella's foot, seeming satisfied.

"What do you..." Through the haze, the realization hits. I'm speaking English. The ghost can't understand me.

I switch to Mandarin, shocked when what comes out instead is the same dialect the ghost is speaking.

"Ning?" This time, when I say it, the words curve differently. The ghost looks up sharply, and hope flutters in my chest. I have her attention. *Are you Ning?* I ask in her language.

She sneers at me.

"Okay, I get it. I'm not fit to say your name," I say. "What do you want?"

The ghost ignores me again, going back to her muttering. But I think back to what Ella said the last time.

Mama, tell her truth.

Not tell *the* truth. Tell *her* truth.

"You want me to tell your truth," I say in the ghost's language. As if in response, the scroll with Ning's story on it crumbles, rot blooming on its surface.

I force myself to focus on the problem as I grab the cast-iron skillet, running toward the gift shop connected to the exhibit hall. I hope like hell that they still have what I remember seeing in the gift shop a year or two ago.

I don't know what Ning's truth is, but I'll figure it out. I have to.

Maybe Sarah knows Ning's real story. The thought crosses my mind as I bash in the gift shop window, breaking up the glass until I can squeeze through.

Oh god, Sarah. I can't think about her now. My heart leaps as I spy the bright red "Write-Your-Own-Ghost-Story Scroll and Brush Pen Kit." Thank goodness for gimmicky gift shop goods. I grab the kit and squeeze back out just as something snaps and Ella screams again.

"No!" I nearly trip in my haste. "I'm going to get you out, Ella. Hang in there, baby girl."

I rip open the kit, tearing the seal on the little ink well and pulling out the blank scroll.

I don't know where to start, so I begin with the theory Sarah and I came up with earlier in the night. She was only pretending not to have a clue about the story. Maybe there's a grain of truth in her 'theory' about Ning's life. I start speaking as I write, expecting the words to come out shaky and blotchy in my unpracticed hand. Instead, they come out perfectly, as if written by a Chinese scholar from the 19th century.

"On the night of the Hungry Ghost Moon, Wu Li, a brilliant scholar, was outside burning offerings for his deceased father. As he spoke a prayer, a young lady and her maid strolled past his garden. At once, he was struck by her beauty and found himself utterly captivated."

The ghost stops and looks up and my heart pounds faster, hope and joy ready to burst forth. It's working! I keep writing, the words tumbling out. I don't change anything until the part describing Ning and Li's married life.

"Ning was a doting wife, filling Li's table with rich meals, tending his household efficiently and respecting his mother. Yet, Li was a horrible husband. He beat Ning and forced her to his bed when she wanted nothing to do with him. As months passed, Li's pallor wanned, and he thinned considerably."

The ghost sneers, and my nerves prickle. *Please don't hurt Ella.* I don't know if the ghost's reaction is a good or bad thing. I continue writing.

"The truth was that Ning was poisoning Li, as he deserved. He died of the poison, and though Ning's mother-in-law suspected, Ning soon gave birth to Li's child, the family's sole heir. Having provided a son, Ning was not punished for her deception, but rather lived on for two decades more. Ning left one day to lay flowers on her mother-in-law's grave and was never seen again."

I set down the brush pen, heart hammering in my chest. "Is that the real story, Ning?"

In response, the ghost howls in rage. A huge gust of wind blows through the museum, bringing with it dark, rotting leaves and picking up shards of glass. I hide my face as a hundred tiny daggers pierce my skin.

Mama! I open my eyes as the ghost bares her teeth, snapping the smallest two toes on my baby girl's foot. Ella's screams ring through my mind and I watch, tears streaming down my face as the ghost grabs a torn silk cloth, pressing Ella's toes under her foot and wrapping the fabric tightly around it.

Abruptly, Ella's screams stop, and I dash toward the mirror, trying to see why she's gone silent, view smeared by my own breath fogging up the glass.

A mixture of horror and relief washes over me as I realize Ella has passed out from pain and trauma.

I stare at the ghost as she ties up the cloth on Ella's left foot, muttering to herself again.

Little girl, I'll be a good mama. Little girl, you won't suffer the way I did. Little girl, you'll be respectable. It'll only hurt a minute. Be still, little girl. Be still.

She moves the washbasin over to Ella's right foot and dips her toes in.

Hell. NO.

"Tell me what you want from me!" I scream at the ghost, who glances up, unconcerned. I look into the hollow

sockets that serve as Ning's eyes, willing her to give me a hint. She tilts her head and smiles. An uncanny, fixed grin like the line painted on a marionette's wooden face.

I hear her voice in my mind.

Ràng wǒ jìn lái.

Let me in.

I recoil. "*Let you in? Why?*"

She tilts her head back the other way, looking somehow disappointed, and goes back to washing Ella's unmutilated foot.

With Ella passed out, my fear hasn't lessened, but without the distraction of her wide, panicked eyes, I finally take a good, long look at the ghost. She wears no jewelry, perhaps because jewelry will no longer stay on her bony limbs. Her thick, unbound hair is twined with long, stringy strands of seaweed. Her tattered gown looks simple and unadorned. No embroidery; nothing like Ning's lavish green, tapered slippers.

The slippers.

I look down to the bony feet peering out from beneath the ghost's gown. To the five unbroken toes on each foot.

The ghost's feet aren't bound.

CHAPTER 9

"**Y**ou're not Ning."

The ghost looks up sharply at me. I have her attention and I can't afford to waste it. I summon every ounce of concentration, speaking my thoughts aloud. I watch the ghost's reaction and keep her focus on me instead of my baby girl's remaining, unbroken foot.

"Only wealthy girls had their feet bound. Poor girls couldn't afford it; they needed to be able to walk to work."

The ghost hasn't moved, still staring at me through two dark eye sockets.

"Ning had bound feet."

I look over at the display case where Ning's green embroidered slippers once sat. They're on the ground now, toppled over and covered with shattered glass.

"And you hated her."

I think back through everything I know. I think back to Ning's story, which I've heard countless times. I stare at the ghost's plain, unadorned robe and five-toed feet.

Ning's dowry included bedding, tea, a sewing kit, jewelry, gold, and...

"You're Ning's maid, aren't you?"

At that, the ghost drops Ella's foot and heads straight for me.

I back away, mind racing. Is she going to cross to this side? Then what?

Think, Jodi! Was there anything else in the story about the maid? No, of course not. No one tells tales about those considered too lowly to matter. How the hell am I supposed to figure out her real story and why she hates Ning so much?

When the ghost reaches the mirror, she reaches her bony hands out toward the surface. As her hands near the glass, her mouth opens, and her gravelly voice repeats the words I first heard in my dream.

Ràng wǒ jìn lái.

Let me in.

Heart hammering, I walk up to the glass, placing my palms over hers. She reaches out and grabs my wrists with inhuman strength. Instinctively, I yank back, fear coursing through me. Have I fallen for a trap? It's too late; her grip overpowers mine.

Ràng wǒ jìn lái.

I glance behind her at Ella, still bound by vines and slumped in the chair. And then I stop fighting, returning my gaze to the ghost. Looking into the hollow where her eyes should be, I bow my head.

"Come in, Good Sister."

She lunges out of the mirror, still holding my hands, and it's everything I can do not to flinch as I hear a strange suction sound when her spirit leaps into my body. Everything grows cold, and one last thought enters my mind before I lose control.

Please let this be the right choice.

***

I'm surrounded by a fuzzy, ethereal landscape, twisted by all the incongruous quirks and alternate dimension rules that belong to the world of the unconscious. But unlike in a typical dream, my mind is clear. Before me I see green fields, rocks carved out by lichen, and beautiful, blooming trees.

Two girls who can't be older than fifteen sit beneath a peach tree, giggling. Both have long, unbound black hair, but one is dressed more lavishly than the other. She has a blossom tucked behind her hair and she reaches out to pluck a juicy peach from the tree, taking a bite.

"Mei," she whispers to the other girl. "Nothing will change once I marry Li. You'll help me run the new household. It'll be just like now. We'll always be sisters."

The other girl—*Mei*—shushes her sister. "*Āiyá*, Ning! Don't let your ma hear you say that!"

Ning laughs, swallowing another bite of the ripe peach. "Ma's just jealous that Ba prefers your ma over her." She looks Mei up and down. "Don't worry. I know you're prettier than me, but *I* don't care about that. Li has money and a big estate with a beautiful garden. If all of it is mine, I don't care whose bed he chooses to share."

Mei's face drains of color.

"Oh, don't worry," Ning says. "I'm sure he'll wait until you're sixteen to take you as a concubine."

The scene begins to shift. For a moment, I can feel my real body again, rooted in the physical world, though I can't see it. I can feel my right arm moving of its own accord, the brush pen from the kit clutched in my fingers.

A new scene materializes. Mei is alone in a room now, pale as a ghost as she huddles under the covers of her bed. She's shivering so hard I think it must be deep winter, until I see that her gaze is fixed on the door to the room. My own heartbeat quickens as the door slides open, revealing a man who looks to be in his late twenties or early thirties.

He steps into the room, closing the door behind him as he approaches Mei. She crawls away from him in the bed, but he crosses the distance in two quick strides and snatches her wrist. The way she flinches from his touch, I know this isn't the first time he's visited her room.

Oh god. I don't want to see this. I try to close my eyes, but I am no longer in control of them. I'm spared what comes next; it seems Mei doesn't want to dwell on this memory either.

The scene turns to one of Mei and Ning whispering in the kitchen. Ning puts her arms around Mei, who's shaken and crying. They whisper so quietly that I can't hear them, but I see Ning slip a pouch to her half-sister. Mei clutches it like a lifeline, and Ning hurries away.

Mei wipes her eyes and begins preparing a meal, rolling out dough for dumplings and filling each one. She tips a bit of powder from the pouch Ning gave her into a few of the dumplings, slicing a tiny cut into the top of each one. Shaking, she hides the powder away and mixes together all the dumplings on a big plate. She brings them out to a table, where Li, Ning, and an older woman who must be Li's mother are seated. Li's eyes follow Mei as she sets the plate on the table before promptly leaving the room.

Ning watches Li, smiling big when he turns back toward her. "Husband! Let me plate your food." She picks up his dish and uses her chopsticks to set food on it. Ning makes a show of listening to his story with great enthusiasm, as she carefully picks out the dumplings with the little cut on top.

The next part of the story I remember from the scroll, where Li's mother calls in a doctor to consult upon a wasting disease, and Li's mother suspects Ning of being a ghost.

As the scene fades, I can feel my hand continue to write, moving down the page. I stop only to dip the brush pen expertly in ink. Vaguely, I wonder where Mei, a lowly serving girl in ancient China, learned to read and write, but I'll probably never know. Maybe she never learned and it's merely an effect of the ghost reality we're in.

This time, Ning and Mei appear in a courtyard, talking under a gingko tree filled with golden leaves. For the first time, Ning looks panicked. Everyone else must be out somewhere, for Ning speaks at a regular volume.

"Mei, they think I'm a ghost, poisoning him!"

Mei laughs bitterly. "If anything, they should think it of me. *I'm* the one whose bed he chose nearly every night before he grew too ill."

She looks bony and pale, hardly the same vibrant girl from the first scene.

Ning glares at her. "This is serious!"

Mei glares back. "I know! I'll stop, but he's already on his deathbed."

"They'll kill me!" Ning wails.

"No, they won't. I won't let them. We'll run away tonight. Don't bring too much, or we'll be weighed down."

Ning frowns, looking down at her slippers with her pointed feet. "You know I can't run fast, like you."

"I'll carry you if I must, and once we're far enough from the village we can use some of the gold from your dowry to bribe a cart-driver for a ride."

"Where will we go?" Ning kicks at the dirt.

"Ma whispered of a secret place where women go to hide," Mei says. "They'll take us in, or we'll find somewhere else. Don't worry. We'll figure it out. We're sisters, after all." She gives Ning's hand a squeeze.

What happened? I wonder, watching the two girls prepare, already heartbroken for whatever comes next. I watch as they carry out their plan, Mei keeping her promise and carrying Ning on her back part of the way. They reach a house tucked away in the mountains, where they're taken in. Both girls promise work for their place there.

They soon discover that Mei is pregnant, and my throat closes up. I wish I could look away, not see any of the pregnancy or her birth, as thoughts of Ella threaten to spill into my mind. *Please don't show me this.*

I don't know if Mei the ghost is listening or has reasons of her own, but the next scene is her holding her baby boy. Despite the ghost's control of my body, I can feel tears spilling from my eyes as I think of holding Ella in the hospital for the first time, her tiny eyes and red face scrunched up in sleep and her hand curled around my finger.

I try hard to concentrate through the sadness as I watch the two sisters sneak out at night, Mei clutching her baby to her chest. Are they running away again?

They reach a clearing by a lake and both of them sit on logs, laughing and talking. Mei looks like she's aged a decade. Ning stares down at her own rough, callused hands. She asks to hold the baby and Mei hands him over. Ning bundles him to her chest and then pulls something out of her pocket.

The knife shimmers in the moonlight right before Ning plunges it forward in one swift motion, stabbing Mei through the chest.

I gasp as Mei sputters and chokes. Her son wakes up and begins squalling.

Ning cries, tears streaming down her cheeks, and it's almost worse than if she were dry-eyed. "I'm sorry, little sister. This is no life for me or for your son. I can't hide from my family forever and work myself into an early death, and what will become of him here? No, we have to go back. He'll be well cared for. I'll raise him as my own. He'll be the legitimate heir to a wealthy family, not the son of a concubine. He'll have a better life than either of us will. I promise."

Mei's son's cries grow louder, and Ning soothes him back to sleep, facing him away from his dying mother. When he won't stop crying, Ning gives up, dragging Mei's body toward the water. She works quickly, filling Mei's pockets with rocks and sewing them shut with a needle from her satchel. She pulls off her belt, tying the rock-filled robe tightly around Mei's body.

I imagine Ning sneaking out for several nights, looking for the perfect, secluded spot. How long did she plan this for?

Groaning with the effort, Ning pushes Mei into the water as the baby starts to wail louder. She coos at him, singing a gentle lullaby as she cleans up the blood and checks for any other evidence that might betray her.

When she's satisfied that she's left no mark, Ning sneaks back to the compound, stopping every so often to rest her aching feet. Back in their room, she hastily grabs their things—hers already packed for the trip—and leaves a note saying she and Mei decided to go home and patch things up with their family.

As Ning sneaks back out again disappearing into the night, I wonder briefly how I'm able to follow what Ning did afterward. How could Mei know what Ning did after dropping her in the lake? Is this Mei's guess at what must have happened?

The answer comes a moment later, from the body we temporarily share. I can feel Mei's boiling anger and resentment, hot enough to keep her in this world as a ghost for over a century. Some Chinese ghosts are tethered to the world by the strength of a grudge, and Mei's is large enough to fill a village.

Mei's rage only grows as she watches Ning present Mei's son as her own. Ning tells her mother-in-law that she discovered Mei was poisoning Li. When she confronted her maid, Mei drugged and kidnapped her to keep her from telling anyone. Ning says that Mei planned to take Ning's son and use him as leverage against the family, but she managed to escape and return home.

Li's mother-in-law, who always liked Ning for her efficiency and obedience as a daughter-in-law, and her willingness to look the other way at Li's affairs, welcomes her back, rejoicing that the family line won't end after all.

Mei's rage keeps her tethered to Ning for a short time, but it's not long before the call of the spirit world pulls at her. She fights to stay, finding a way to take her revenge, but it is only on Ghost Day when she can reach into the living world.

One Ghost Day, when Ning goes to lay offerings on her mother-in-law's grave, Mei finally gets her vengeance, but even Ning's death doesn't release Mei. Every Ghost Day, she watches her son honor and mourn Ning.

When her son dies, Mei's strength begins to fade. Still, her descendants continue to pass down the story of Ning, and it's enough to stoke Mei's continuing wrath. Strange things happen often enough to Mei's living family that they begin to believe they have a strong connection with the ghost world.

Her anger is kicked up again when her own descendants, Sarah's family, put up an entire exhibit honoring Ning, for all the world to see. Mei wreaks thoughtless havoc the first two Ghost Days at the garden, but on the third, she bides her time until evening, when she lures a child into the water.

My own rage feels ready to burst as I realize that Ella's death was no accident; Mei took her from me. But it's also mixed in with all of Mei's emotions, and I feel like I'm going to pass out from the intensity of everything running through me.

Lastly, I see me and Sarah setting up the altars and the feast. Mei is finally able to fully enter the living realm when Sarah and I invite her in with our delicious rice cakes and offerings.

I put up an altar for Ella and brought her into contact with our world.

Sarah burnt an offering for her ancestors, and Mei answered.

***

I collapse to the ground with the shock of Mei leaving me. Glass shards dig into my arms and back. I force myself to sit up, despite the pain and exhaustion. *Think about Ella.*

I look in the mirror, where Ella still lies passed out on the chair, but the vines tied around her have receded. My gaze turns toward the ghost. Instead of the rotting, decaying thing, she looks like Mei from the visions; a teen girl who got the worst end of what life has to offer. She looks stricken, but as I watch, her face melts into relief. I realize that other than Mei's murderer, I'm the first person to know the truth of her story.

There's a new scroll on the floor in front of me, filled with Mei's story. It looks perfectly aged, like the original scroll of Ning's story, and I marvel. I can read it, but it takes effort, unlike the ease of conversation I've been having with Mei.

I look around. The glass displays are still shattered, perhaps because they were broken by Sarah's hand, not Mei's, but the building looks solid again, with only a touch of the pervading rot. I know, instinctively, that this time, the garden will let us out.

With Mei's story told, her power must be fading.

Mei goes to pick up Ella, no longer threatening to break her toes, and puts her arms around my baby girl. I think about what it must have been like for Mei, thrown into one horrible situation after another by circumstances beyond her control. And then her half-sister, her best friend, the one person she thought would always be on her side, betrayed her in the worst ways possible.

I wonder what kind of person could do that.

I wonder how Ning lived all those years with the heaviest kind of secret, never speaking a word of what she'd done.

I wonder.

And then a terrible idea begins to form.

It's growing harder to speak Mei's language, and the words come out garbled and slow as sinking mud, but I speak them before I can think twice.

Mei, wait! I want to make a bargain.

CHAPTER 10

Moss peers up through cracks between stones on the pathway as I drag Sarah's body out into the garden, my teeth clenched around a knife handle. The water has receded, the soil damp but no longer muddy. I can hear the whisper of soft ground cover creeping back in to reclaim its rightful space, covering up the dead grass and black sludge littering the courtyard. Green leaves sprout on bare branches, and old, displaced leaves blow away in tiny gusts as though swept aside by an unseen hand. As Sarah and I pass a waist-height shrub, tiny buds begin to sprout from the tips of its twig-like branches. At this rate, the garden will be whole again by sunrise.

Sarah takes a deep breath as if she can feel the fresh air fill her lungs, even in her unconscious state.

My muscles ache as I drag her across the stone footbridge, peering down at the dark water below, where fish splash around, weaving around one another in playful half-circles. I could have wheeled her out here, but it didn't feel right. I shouldn't be allowed to make this any easier on myself. Or maybe I knew carrying her out myself would be harder and take longer.

Giving me more time to back out.

Despite my best efforts, her body thumps along the ground as we hit an uneven patch of packed earth, and I wince.

Sorry, Sarah. We're almost there.

In a small clearing shielded from the rest of the garden by a copse of trees, I set Sarah down gently. Her eyelids are still closed, but her neck remains rigid, and her head doesn't relax to either side. If she opens her eyes, she'll be looking straight into the night sky. Smears of dirt and slime speckle her t-shirt and her thick, jet-black hair is full of twigs. She looks enchanting, like a forest faerie from a folktale. I set the knife on the ground and brush the hair from her forehead before planting a kiss.

"I'm sorry, Sarah," I whisper. Then I pull her shirt up, exposing her half-moon stomach, hold my arm out above her, and slash my wrist with the knife.

I hiss in pain, dropping the knife next to me, but I don't move my other arm. Warm blood drips onto Sarah's stomach, oozing down the slope of her rounded belly. I see little flickers of motion inside as Baby Henry kicks frantically.

I want to look away, but I force myself to keep my gaze on Sarah, peering at her through lidded eyes.

"I've done my part," I whisper, words meant for Mei, though I no longer know which language I speak. *"Your turn."*

Vines curl up out of the ground as I draw back my wrist, binding it with a bandage I took from the first aid kit. With only one hand and my teeth to bind it, the cloth wraps around me, awkward and uneven. My mind travels back to earlier and Sarah's gentle, soft touch as she carefully dabbed ointment on my head wound.

With the hand that wielded the knife, I reach out for Sarah's cold fingers, wrapping them up in mine. Every part of me screams to look away, to leave, to wait until it's over before coming back to see what consequences my bargain has wrought; but I stay put. I owe it Sarah to bear witness to what I've done.

To what I'm about to do to her.

As I watch, the vines grow thorns, thickening until they resemble a sharp bramble. They look out of place in a Chinese garden, an invasive species come to kill the pretty, delicate plants that belong here. Hearty vines curl up around my best friend, and for a moment, I'm terrified they'll tear through the fabric covering her crotch. Would I stop them then? Would I be able to?

But they leave her clothing intact, instead growing around her, reaching up over her exposed stomach. When they reach the top, they stop.

My bandaged wrist throbs painfully as my eyes flick toward the knife. Will I need to make the incision?

While I hesitate, a thorn on the tip of one vine grows, curving wicked and sharp like a dagger. Bile fills my mouth as it slices a line down Sarah's abdomen. There's pressure on my palm, and I look down to see Sarah's knuckles turn white. Still unconscious, she squeezes my hand, as if some part of her knows what's happening.

Rivulets of tears run down my face as I murmur useless apologies, my head growing light as I watch the vines dig into the cut. Like tentacles, they curl around something inside, pulling it out with triumph.

It's wrapped in leaves, stained crimson.

Sarah's nails dig into my skin and I welcome the pain, whispering more apologies. The largest vine remains while the rest recede into the earth, trailing droplets of red where they retract. All that remains is the sacrifice, still hidden inside stained foliage.

A breeze cuts through the air and I swear the moon grows brighter for a moment. Through the trees I see colorful flowers blooming all around, the vibrant joy of the garden. I have the distinct impression that the courtyard is shaking with happy laughter.

Near the vine, a small hole opens up in the earth. Sarah cries out as the last stalk plunges down into the soil, taking its sacrifice with it.

I hate myself for the little wellspring of hope that blooms in my chest.

And then a fresh wave of guilt hits. I look down at Sarah, grateful that her eyes are closed, grateful that she wasn't awake for my betrayal. I wonder if she'll die from her wounds, wonder if there's anything I can do to save her. But as I watch, her skin knits itself back together, the bump of her belly no longer taut and full. It sags in the middle, and nothing kicks inside. I hold her hand as tears run down both our faces.

Until a voice calls from somewhere behind me.

"Mama?"

CHAPTER 11

"Mom, is that you?" Sarah's eyes flutter open, blinking hard when she sees me instead of her mother.

"Hey, Sarah," I keep my voice as soft and soothing as I can manage. "It's Jodi. Your mom was here earlier, but she had to leave to attend to business at the garden. Don't worry. I said I'd keep you company."

Sarah takes this in, looking around and absorbing the steel-gray walls and beeping machines. The various tubes attached to her and her blue paisley hospital gown. Her brows furrow. "What... what happened?"

"What's the last thing you remember?" I ask, keeping my tone steady.

She blinks several times. "I... um. I don't know. I think I was making rice cakes for... something? Ghost Day?"

I sigh. "That's last year's Ghost Day memory, Sarah. You did the catering for the garden, remember?"

"Um... yeah. I think so."

"So, you don't remember deciding to go into the Museum at night to work on the newest acquisition?" I prod.

She shakes her head, the movement making her grimace. "I... have a headache."

I reach out to touch her arm and she flinches back.

"Sorry." She sounds sheepish.

"It's okay," I assure her. "Anyone would be jumpy after getting attacked by an intruder." Sarah's eyes widen as I continue. "From what the police and your family can gather, you went into the office. They said you'd been excited about a new acquisition. A thief broke in, expecting to be alone. They started smashing up the exhibits, trying to steal some of the artifacts. You heard the noise and ran down. Startled, they must have struck you. But it seems they had a conscience, since they called the cops anonymously to let them know there was someone injured on the property. You were found in the middle of the exhibit hall, surrounded by broken glass."

It used nearly all the strength I had left to drag Sarah back into the museum, but it fit the narrative more cleanly. Besides, I don't want anyone looking too closely at that spot in the garden. Who knows what they'll find?

"Oh." Sarah takes all of this in, still looking disoriented.

"It's not all bad news, though. While inventorying the office upstairs to ensure nothing else had been taken, your family found another scroll, dated back to the same time period as Ning's story. It contains the story of Mei, her half-sister, and talks of a betrayal. If the story is true, Mei is your direct ancestor, not Ning. The scroll names the lake where Mei was supposedly drowned. Your dad is working on verifying the authenticity of the scroll; he knows the exhibits mean a lot to you and wants to take you to China with him once you've recovered, if you're interested. To look for Mei's bones."

"Oh," Sarah says again, nodding. "That sounds... good." Then she frowns. "But I can't get on a plane during the third trimester..." I watch as panic hits her eyes, the realization striking. "What about the baby? Is Henry okay?" Her hand reaches down to touch her stomach, feeling the folds of her loose skin. She presses tighter, waiting for the reassuring pressure of a tiny foot kicking. She looks up at me hopefully. "Was he born early? Is he in the ICU?"

I don't have to fake the way my face falls, a mirror of her own, when I don't reply immediately. I know exactly what it feels like to wake up and realize that your child is gone. She crumples into the sheets, sobbing so hard her

102

nose begins running, tears and snot staining her pillow. I pull the blanket up over her back, exposed as it is by the flimsy nightgown, and hold her hand as she weeps, new tears continuing to drip down her red, blotchy face long past the time when they should have run out.

I know what that feels like too, and self-loathing curls a hard knot in my stomach.

The curtains pull open and two heads peek in. Anton, holding Ella, looks at Sarah, whose back is turned toward the door. He makes a wincing face that's easy to read. *Oops, I'll come back later.* I wave him off even as worry tightens my throat when he and Ella turn to leave. I owe it to Sarah not to remind her that she's just lost her child when I still have mine, but I don't know if I'll ever get over the panic of having Ella out of my sight. My eyes trail my little girl, who is healthy and whole, except for four broken toes. They're in a cast now, and we're carrying her everywhere for a while.

Right before they leave, Ella asks Anton, "Is Sawah okay?"

Sarah turns, wiping her blotchy face, and calls out. "I'm okay, Ella." She clears her throat, trying to shake away the wobble. "Come say hi to Sarah *Āyí.*"

I watch my best friend compose herself enough to smile at my four-year-old girl, right after she's received the most devastating news of her life.

I think about how much easier it would be to forget and forgive myself if I walked away from Sarah forever. How I might someday be able to convince myself that this was all a dream, to let Sarah fade slowly from my heart and my memories.

But I keep in mind the bargain I made with Mei.

"I will give you a baby boy of your own bloodline, one who is unborn and hasn't been told lies. He'll be like a son to you. Ella will never forget me, her rightful mother, but this child won't know any other. You can be his true mother."

Mei baring her teeth in return. *"And why should I give something that's mine in exchange for something that isn't yours to give?"*

"Because I'll make sure you can keep him forever. Ensure his mother never knows what happened, never comes back to the garden to try to get her little boy back. And I'll make sure your story is told. Sarah and her family might not believe the truth of your story without prodding, but I'll make sure they do. I will convince your descendants to pay their respects to you, their rightful ancestor, and reveal Ning for the traitor she was. I can plant the suggestion for them to find your bones and give you a proper burial; or if they can't or won't find it, I'll look for them myself. You've had a hard life, and a harder afterlife, Mei. I'll help you rest in peace. Let me have Ella back, and you'll have everything you ever wanted."

Mei's long sigh as she imagined truly being at rest. And then the one word that will reverberate forever through my bones.

"Deal."

No one seems to remember that Ella died for a year. To them, she's always been alive and I'm just an over-protective mom. To them, her speech is slightly delayed for a four-year-old and she seems to have developed night terrors, but everyone figures both might be a way of coping with the trauma of her toes breaking when she and I fell into a ravine while out hiking. The same trip where I got the injury on the back of my head. Odd, how her big toe didn't break along with the rest, but stranger things have happened.

I hug Sarah, promising her I'll come with her to China when she's well again, if she wants. Telling her we can honor her baby with a ceremony. That when she recovers, I'll train for a half-marathon with her.

"When I first woke up, I could've sworn..." She shakes her head. "For a moment I had no idea who you were or how we met." She claps her hand over her mouth. "God, what an awful thing to say. Here you are, being an amazing friend, and I'm sniveling like the world's biggest idiot."

"Sarah," I say with a light laugh. "Come on, it's fine! To say you've had a rough few days would be a massive understatement. You're allowed to be a little frazzled right now."

She sags in relief, looking at me with wide, grateful eyes. "I'm so lucky to have you as a friend, Jodi."

"I'm your best friend," I say. "And I always will be."

THE END

AFTERWORD

Sometimes, I envy those who've spent most of their lives immersed in horror. The aficionados who can list every famous slasher villain in order from favorite to least (with strong opinions on which sequels to skip), who ritualistically reread their favorite King novel each year, and who transform their front yards into bloody crime scenes every Halloween. While I've read my fair share of Goosebumps, have a long-standing appreciation for the Gothic, and have always been drawn to the aesthetics of the macabre, truth is, horror was just another genre to me...until it reached out a ghostly hand when I needed it most.

It was mid-November. Things were rough in the larger world, but my narrow little corner was in decent shape, considering. The words were flowing in my mystery novel manuscript, my happy, healthy toddler was a month from turning two, and my husband and I were about to announce to friends and family that our second child was on the way.

Then the bleeding began.

It took two weeks, numerous blood tests and other invasive procedures, and a lot of heartache to confirm that I was, indeed, miscarrying.

I stopped writing. I focused on cooking and baking for the holidays. I cried a lot. I did whatever I could to stay distracted. Weeks of not writing turned into over a month (a long stretch for my restless writer's brain); still, there were no words. By the time the new year rolled around, I recognized that I could not return to the manuscript I'd so eagerly begun. But I'd spent half a year researching, planning, and drafting that novel. If not that, then, what?

On a cold January morning, I sat at my kitchen counter with my laptop open, staring down the blank page. Instead of picking up one of my existing ideas, I let myself write whatever came to mind. The result was a short story typed out in one or two feverish sessions—a raw mess of emotions shaped like a narrative. In it, a strange, rust red creature escapes from a woman's bleeding body and begins to grow. It was my first-ever horror story: a tale of psychological torture and pain that ends with a tiny fragment of hope. Typing out the last words, I felt a mixture of sadness, pride in having finally written *something*, and overwhelming, nearly all-consuming, much-welcomed relief.

I was hooked.

From there, I sought out more horror. More inspiration. More experiences that helped me tackle my many anxieties head-on. I read. I watched. I wrote. I pored through Chinese folklore tales, delighted by the abundance of vengeful ghosts, murderous demons, and vicious creatures found within. Thanks to recommendations from friends well-versed in the genre, I discovered the beautiful art form that is the horror novella—and the desire to write one began calling to me.

As is my usual process, I started actively brainstorming. Idea after idea crossed my mind, but nothing felt right. Every concept felt too cautious. For that first story, I hadn't chosen vulnerability; it's just what escaped when I didn't let myself think too hard. I wasn't sure how to go about tackling horror in an intentional way.

Finally, frustrated by the umpteenth not-quite-right idea, I asked my husband for help. He's a thoughtful, reserved guy who doesn't impose; but when pressed, he often shares incredibly insightful advice. He listened to all my ideas. And he noticed—as only someone close to me could—that I'd shied away from the things I was most anxious about. The thoughts that keep me up at night, that intrude on my mind regularly, that drive me to panic if I spend too much time with them. He suggested I lean into the fear.

Hell no, I said. But then I thought about it.

From that conversation, *Bound Feet* was born. I poured all my love for my toddler daughter—and my constant concerns for her safety—into this book. I mixed in the still-raw grief from my miscarriage, and my worries about what might happen to my marriage if we were to go through a trauma as deep as Jodi's and Anton's. I mixed bits of Chinese ghost folklore—inspired by my research—into the story. I researched foot binding and, through a conversation with my dad, discovered that my great-grandmother had bound feet. And I set my story at an invented Chinese garden, inspired in-part by the venue where my husband and I held our wedding reception.

Bound Feet is a mix of some of the best and worst moments in my life; my greatest joys and my greatest fears. It's a love letter in the form of a bloody, beating heart. If you're new to horror, it's the ghostly hand I'm reaching out to you; if you're a seasoned connoisseur, it's my humble offering to a thriving, wonderful genre. Thank you for reading.

ACKNOWLEDGMENTS

In November 2015, one of my favorite authors shared a post about their participation in National Novel Writing Month. Writing a book had always been a "someday" dream of mine, and the event sounded fun. On a whim, I began drafting my first manuscript.

In the nearly seven years that have passed since that day, I've been immensely fortunate in the wealth of support I've received. It would be impossible to name every kind individual, but if you've helped me in my journey, thank you. I would like to acknowledge a few people in particular.

First, to Sadie Hartmann and Joe Sullivan, who have taken this story—one that's incredibly precious to me—and treated it with more care than I could ever have dreamt possible. I've said this before, but it remains true: I still can't believe I get to publish my debut book with you two incredible champions at the helm.

My huge thanks to Luke Spooner for the stunning cover and Ryan Mills for the beautiful title page. Both of you went above and beyond for this book. I'm honored to have illustrations by such talented, skilled artists grace my debut. And to everyone who blurbed *Bound Feet*, reviewed an early copy, or spread the word about my book release, thank you.

Thank you to my brilliant critique partners, whose sharp eyes have helped me improve countless stories, including this one. Without each of you, weathering the long road to publication would've been infinitely less bearable. Jena Brown, my horror BFF and the first person I'd call for help if a body needed burying. CG Drews, the other half of my brain, who always knows the perfect thing to say to make me laugh when I feel like crying. Seline DuMane, my writing sprint partner and a tireless cheerleader who's always there to lend a helping hand. And Eleanor Thomas, my fellow gothic-and-dark-academia queen and one of my first writing friends. Seline and Ellie, our group chat brings me endless joy.

A wonderful fleet of beta readers helped me shape *Bound Feet* into the story it is now. In addition to my critique partners above and family members to follow, thank you to Carl Laviolette, Emily Lawhorn, Ashley Saywers, Sarah Chen, Maranda Medina, Christine Lee, Erin Hartel, Bilan Todd, Krizelle DeGuzman, Carina Saal, Tara Hansen, Andrea Aquino, Samantha Hunt, and Carolyn Brooks. Thank you for taking the time and care in reading my manuscript and offering your feedback. Any mistakes remaining are mine.

A special shoutout to all the members of The Happy Place and to my book club friends for their constant support. And to all the friends who have supported my career—whether we met as kids or more recently, in person or online: I'm grateful for you, and for the community, friendship, and help you've provided. If you've critiqued a piece of mine, cheered me on, or provided support in any one of myriad other ways: my sincerest thanks for your help on this journey.

My husband, Tal, has made so many sacrifices for my pursuit of this dream. He was the one who encouraged me to quit my full-time accounting job in order to spend more time writing, knowing (and not caring) that our finances would take a hit. He spends much of his time on evenings and weekends doing housework, cooking for us, and watching our kids—anything he can to help me carve out a little more writing time. He took my career seriously before I dared admit how much it meant to me, and he's helped me with every piece I've written. Everything from brainstorming over dinner to solving story problems to reading messy first drafts to cheering me up when things go wrong and making sure I celebrate when they go right. It's no exaggeration to say that without him, this book wouldn't exist.

I'm lucky to have a remarkable base of support among the rest of our family members—our kids, my parents and siblings, my in-laws, and our extended family—who encouraged me to pursue my dreams and continued to ask about my writing long before I had anything to show for it, who read versions of various manuscripts, and who gifted me research books or let me pick their brains about something relevant to a story. I can't wait to have cake and celebrate the book release with all of you.

And last but never least, my mom, to whom this book is dedicated. Thank you for reading every story of mine and sharing your insight, for watching the little ones while I work on various manuscripts, and for embracing horror—even though it made you nervous at first—because I started writing it. I'm eternally grateful that you reminded me often of how much you loved *Bound Feet*—and encouraged me to submit it to My Dark Library when I was afraid my words might not be worthy enough. You're my model for motherhood; if, in a decade or two, my kids look up to me half as much as I look up to you, I'll consider it a job well done.

ABOUT THE AUTHOR

Kelsea Yu is a Chinese and Taiwanese American writer who lives in Seattle with her husband and children. Whether through a speculative or real-world lens, her writing explores diaspora identity, twists on folklore, complicated interpersonal relationships, and characters who make unconventional choices.

Kelsea's debut novella, *Bound Feet*, is forthcoming from Cemetery Gates Media. She also has stories forthcoming in *Reckoning* and in various anthologies, including *Classic Monsters Unleashed*, *Death in the Mouth*, and *Dark Matter Presents: Human Monsters*. Kelsea is represented by Jen Azantian of Azantian Literary Agency.

*Check out other **My Dark Library** titles at*
MyDarkLibrary.com

#1 *Stargazers* – LP Hernandez

#2 *#thighgap* – Chandler Morrison

#3 *Bound Feet* – Kelsea Yu

#4 *Taboo in Four Colors* – Tim McGregor

#5 *The Bonny Swans* – P.L. Watts

#6 *Corporate Body* – R.A. Busby